## *Stephanie Searches for Her Destiny Guy*

"There's a perfect guy for every girl. He's out there somewhere, waiting for her," Stephanie declared.

"But how do they find each other?" Anna asked. "What if the girl is from South America and the boy is from the North Pole?"

"They'd have to have some kind of radar," Allie teased.

"Mayday! Mayday!" Darcy pretended to be speaking into a shortwave radio. "Perfect guy spotted at twelve o'clock on the radar screen. Over."

Stephanie rolled her eyes. Her friends just weren't getting it, but she knew she was right.

"Okay, Steph, maybe you are right," Allie conceded. "Maybe there *is* some kind of destiny at work when it comes to love. Then why don't we stop worrying about meeting boys? I mean, if fate is going to bring us to them anyway?"

Stephanie shook her head. "Just because one guy is your destiny doesn't mean you can't blow it! Or that nothing can get in your way. You can't be lazy about it—you have to nudge fate along.

"That's it!" she announced, gazing at her three friends. "That's what I'm going to do this summer."

Darcy, Anna, and Allie exchanged puzzled looks. "What?" Anna asked.

"Find my perfec[illegible]ed. "That's my project fo[illegible] to look for my Mr. Perfe[illegible]

**FULL HOUSE™: Stephanie novels**

Phone Call from a Flamingo
The Boy-Oh-Boy Next Door
Twin Troubles
Hip Hop Till You Drop
Here Comes the Brand-New Me
The Secret's Out
Daddy's Not-So-Little Girl
P.S. Friends Forever
Getting Even with the Flamingoes
The Dude of My Dreams
Back-to-School Cool
Picture Me Famous
Two-for-One Christmas Fun
The Big Fix-up Mix-up
Ten Ways to Wreck a Date
Wish Upon a VCR
Doubles or Nothing
Sugar and Spice Advice
Never Trust a Flamingo
The Truth About Boys
Crazy About the Future
My Secret Secret Admirer
Blue Ribbon Christmas
The Story On Older Boys
My Three Weeks as a Spy
No Business Like Show Business

*Club Stephanie:*

#1 Fun, Sun, and Flamingoes
#2 Fireworks and Flamingoes
#3 Flamingo Revenge
#4 Too Many Flamingoes

Available from MINSTREL Books

# Too Many Flamingoes

**Based on the hit Warner Bros. TV series**

**Lisa Eisenberg**

A Parachute Book

Published by POCKET BOOKS
New York London Toronto Sydney Tokyo Singapore

A MINSTREL PAPERBACK *ORIGINAL*

A Minstrel Book published by
POCKET BOOKS, a division of Simon & Schuster Inc.
1230 Avenue of the Americas, New York, NY 10020

A PARACHUTE BOOK

ISBN: 0-671-02122-2

First Minstrel Books printing June 1998

10 9 8 7 6 5 4 3 2 1



Cover art by Schultz Photography

Printed in the U.S.A.

# Too Many Flamingoes

# CHAPTER 1

"Why aren't there any guys left?" Stephanie Tanner complained. She folded the last crease in the paper airplane she was making. She threw it across the room, flopped onto her bed, and sighed.

"You mean anywhere in the world?" her best friend Darcy Powell teased.

Allie Taylor, Stephanie's other best friend, glanced up from the fashion magazine she was flipping through. "I could have sworn I saw a guy this morning," she commented, pretending to look puzzled.

"Oh, no! Do you think some alien kidnapped all the guys and brought them back to some 'guyless' planet?" Darcy said in a terrified voice.

Stephanie tossed her pillow at her friends, who

both giggled. "You know what I mean," she said, sitting up. "There aren't any guys *to like*."

Darcy sat beside Stephanie on the bed. "It's true. You haven't really liked anyone since Rick moved away," she said. Rick and Stephanie had dated the past summer, but now that his family had moved, he and Stephanie could only be pen pals. "But that doesn't mean you're never going to meet anyone else."

"Why can't I meet someone like *him?*" Stephanie pointed to the huge poster tacked up over her bed. It showed a tall, dark-haired teenage boy with intense blue eyes. The boy was standing on a stage, singing into a microphone.

Darcy stared at the poster in disbelief. "You want to meet Zack? Of Zack and the Zees? You're dreaming!"

"He *is* the cutest guy in the universe," Stephanie pointed out.

"Right," Allie agreed. "And a major rock star. Which is why you'll never meet him."

"It's not impossible," Stephanie declared.

"Oh, no?" Darcy and Allie exchanged doubtful looks.

"No." Stephanie leaned back and gazed at the poster dreamily. "I could get front row seats for one of Zack's concerts. He'd run onstage and glance into the crowd. Our eyes would meet—and he'd say, 'There she is! There's the girl who's meant for me!' "

"Or he'd say, 'There's the girl they should take to the nuthouse!' " Darcy grinned, tossing her dark hair over one shoulder. Her black eyes sparkled with her teasing.

Allie giggled. "Now, *that* is totally possible," she agreed.

Darcy burst out laughing.

Stephanie giggled with them. She didn't mind their teasing. It seemed as if the three of them had been best friends practically forever. Together, they made a perfect team.

Stephanie rose and went over to plop down on her desk chair. "Okay, I don't have to meet the *actual* Zack—just a boy who is like him," she said. "Somebody tall and cute with blue eyes and wavy dark hair. Someone into music, and a really good singer, and . . ."

"At least you're keeping an open mind," Allie joked.

There was a loud knock at the bedroom door.

"Who could that be?" Allie asked.

"It's Zack!" Darcy squealed. She jumped to her feet and then did an exaggerated swoon onto the bed. The door opened and Anna Rice walked in. Stephanie, Darcy, and Allie had met Anna only the past summer, but they felt as if she were a lifelong friend now.

Anna's freckled face broke into a puzzled grin. "What are you screaming about?" she asked. "I could hear you all the way down the hall."

"Rock stars," Darcy replied. "Cute boy rock stars."

"Do we always have to talk about boys?" Anna complained.

"You don't fool us," Stephanie told her. "You like to talk about boys just as much as we do."

Anna smiled. She pushed her long, dark hair behind her shoulder. "I guess you're right."

"Hey! You streaked your hair last night," Darcy said.

Anna nodded. "It looks great," Allie commented, admiring Anna's coppery highlights.

"Thanks. The best part about it is, it's only temporary," Anna explained. She went over and examined herself in the mirror on Stephanie's dresser. "It washes out when you shampoo. I think I'm going to try a different color next time."

"You could coordinate your hair color to match your outfits," Allie joked.

Anna laughed. "Yeah, instead of painting on paper and canvases I can paint my hair."

Anna was the artistic one in the group. She made

her own jewelry, painted murals for her room, and sewed the colorful clothing that she loved to wear.

"Hey—no one mentioned my new earrings." Darcy tucked her hair behind her ears to show off the silver hoops that gleamed against her dark skin.

"Gorgeous. Totally cover-girl material," Anna told her. "In fact, we're all looking good."

"Then we should definitely be able to find guys this summer," Stephanie said. "But not just any guys—" She stopped talking as her five-year-old cousin dashed through the open bedroom door.

"Nicky!" Stephanie exclaimed as he threw himself onto her lap. A second later Nicky was followed by his twin brother, Alex.

"What are you two doing in here?" Stephanie tickled them until they screamed with laughter. "Isn't it your bath time?"

"It sure is!" Stephanie's uncle Jesse appeared in the doorway. He scowled at the boys. "I thought I told you two to behave—or no cookies after your bath!"

"We don't want a bath, Daddy," Nicky told him.

Jesse picked up Nicky and tucked him under one arm. "Sorry, sport. Your mother said it's bath time, so no arguing."

Uncle Jesse and his friend Joey Gladstone had moved into the Tanner house shortly after Stephanie's mother died—when Stephanie was just a little girl. Stephanie's dad, Danny Tanner, needed help raising his three daughters. Besides Stephanie, he had to look after her older sister, D.J., and her younger sister, Michelle.

A few years earlier, Jesse married Becky Donaldson and they had the twins. Now they lived in the attic apartment. With four adults, five kids, and one dog in the house, things got pretty wild at times.

Alex scooted off Stephanie's lap and tried to run past Jesse. "No bath!" he yelled.

"Got you!" Stephanie's aunt Becky dashed into the room just in time to capture Alex. Her long, dark hair fell over her eyes as she scooped Alex into her arms.

"Here, honey, I'll take him," Jesse told her. "It's my turn anyway. I'll give these wild animals their bath." He snatched Alex away from Becky and leaned over to give her a kiss. Becky gazed dreamily into his eyes.

"Thanks, sweetheart," she said.

"There!" Stephanie declared as Jesse left the room. "That's exactly what I mean."

"What?" Allie gave her a baffled look. Anna and Darcy stared at her in confusion.

"The perfect guy!" Stephanie turned to Becky. "Don't you think that you and Uncle Jesse were meant to be together? Like, it was fate that you found each other?"

Becky smiled. "It does feel that way," she said. "I guess that's how you always feel when you're in love."

"Then you always knew Uncle Jesse was *the* guy for you, right?" Stephanie asked.

Becky laughed. "I'm not sure when I knew," she admitted. "But it didn't take long. The first moment I saw him, I got this . . . I felt this . . . you know, it's like . . ." She shrugged. "I don't know how to describe it," she finally said. "But you'll know, Steph, when it happens to you." She checked her watch. "I'd better help Jesse. The boys *do* become wild animals when they get into the bathtub." She hurried out of the room.

"See?" Stephanie told her friends. "Becky and Jesse really *are* a perfect match. They were meant to be together. It was fate."

"Yeah, I guess they got lucky," Darcy said.

"No—luck had nothing to do with it," Stephanie told her. "Don't you see what Becky meant? There's a perfect guy for every girl. He's out there somewhere waiting for her."

"But how do they find each other?" Anna asked. "What if the girl is from South America and the boy is from the North Pole?"

"They'd have to have some kind of radar," Allie teased.

"Mayday! Mayday!" Darcy pretended to be speaking into a shortwave radio. "Perfect guy spotted at twelve o'clock on the radar screen. Over."

"Think of the frequent flyer miles you'd rack up trying to find him," Anna joked.

"You guys," Stephanie protested. "I'm serious. I really think there is someone fated for each of us. And if a relationship is truly meant to be, the two people will find each other. Even if one of them is at the North Pole."

Darcy shook her head. "I really hope my Mr. Perfect isn't Santa Claus or an elf."

"But, Darcy, think of the *presents*," Allie pointed out, then laughed again.

Stephanie rolled her eyes. Her friends just weren't getting it, but she knew she was right. She knew that her aunt Becky and uncle Jesse were the perfect couple because they were perfect for each other, and fate had brought them together.

"Okay, Steph, maybe you're right," Allie conceded. "Maybe there is some kind of destiny at work when it comes to love. Then why don't we stop worrying about meeting boys? I mean, if fate is going to bring them to us anyway?"

Stephanie shook her head. "Just because one guy is your destiny doesn't mean you can't blow it! Or that nothing can get in your way. You can't be lazy about it—you have to nudge fate along.

"That's it!" she announced, gazing at her three friends. "That's what I'm going to do this summer."

Darcy, Anna, and Allie exchanged puzzled looks. "What?" Anna asked.

"Find my perfect guy," Stephanie declared. "That's my project for the summer. I am going to look for my Mr. Perfect!"

"Oh, no, you won't!" Stephanie and her friends glanced up in surprise as Kayla Norris burst into the room.

Kayla was the fifth member of their group—their "club," as Stephanie thought of it. Kayla had also met the girls the past summer and become an instant friend. Now her cheeks were flushed as if she'd been running hard. Her long, blond hair was falling out of its thick braid, but her brown eyes were sparkling with excitement.

"I know exactly how we're all spending the summer," Kayla announced. "Wait till you hear what I just did!"

# CHAPTER 2

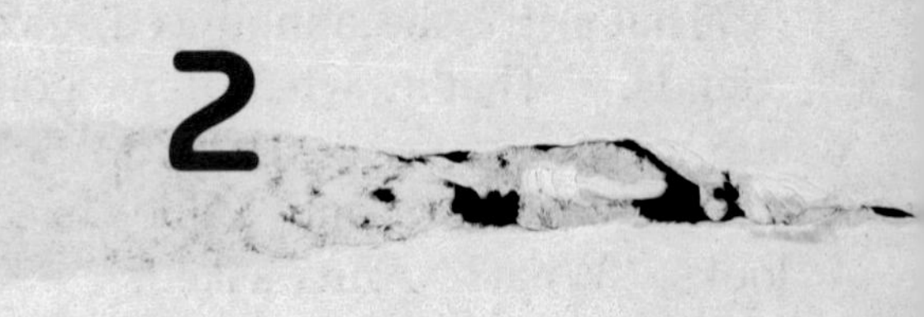

Kayla sank onto the edge of Stephanie's bed and fanned herself with a sheet of bright orange paper. "I ran all the way," she said. "I couldn't wait to tell you about it."

"Tell us about what?" Stephanie demanded.

"What did you do?" Anna asked. Darcy and Allie crowded next to Kayla, waiting for her answer.

"I signed us up for the best thing ever." Kayla showed them the sheet of orange paper.

" 'Summer Sail for Teens,' " Stephanie read out loud. " 'Join the crew aboard the eighty-foot schooner *Sunshine*. Classes sponsored by the Golden Gate Yacht Club, held at the Golden Gate Marina. No experience necessary. All welcome.' "

"Isn't it great?" Kayla practically exploded with excitement. "We'll actually learn how to sail!"

Darcy leaned in closer for a better look at the flyer. "Sailing? Awesome! I've always wanted to learn to sail," she exclaimed. "It's supposed to be really hard but really cool too."

Darcy was the most athletic member of the group. Stephanie admired the way she was always looking for new challenges. But now Stephanie was uncertain. "But we haven't decided what to do this summer, remember?"

"Yeah," Anna told Kayla. "I thought we were going back to the community center to run our day camp again. You know we were invited back."

"And we loved running the camp last summer," Allie pointed out. "Working with our little campers was great."

"Oh, really?" Kayla asked. "Did you guys forget all the trouble we had? Like how the Flamingoes tried to get us kicked out of the pool?"

*Ugh,* Stephanie thought. Just thinking about the Flamingoes irritated Stephanie. They were a group of rich, pretty, popular girls who went to her school. They were also incredible snobs—and mean.

Sure, the Flamingoes dressed in great clothes, and they acted friendly enough—if they needed something from you. But if they didn't need you, or if you got between them and something they wanted—watch out!

The Flamingoes were Stephanie's worst enemies. They were always playing dirty tricks on her and her friends.

"Now that you mention it, the Flamingoes are a very good reason *not* to go back to the community center," Stephanie admitted. "A very good reason."

"Yeah, and if we joined Summer Sail, we could keep all the guys at the marina for ourselves," Kayla added.

"Guys? What guys? Let me see that thing!" Stephanie grabbed the orange flyer from Kayla. "Why didn't you say that Summer Sail is co-ed!"

"Of course it is," Kayla replied. "Just think—we'll get to spend the whole month of June on a boat with a bunch of cute new guys!"

"Maybe even Mr. Perfect," Darcy teased.

"Mr. who?" Kayla asked, confused.

Darcy laughed. "Oh, Stephanie has this idea that there's a destiny guy out there just waiting for her."

Stephanie felt her face heat up. It sounded sort of dumb the way Darcy put it, but Stephanie truly believed she was right.

"I totally think that, too," Kayla said. "What else is love at first sight? It's coming face-to-face with the boy who was meant for you."

"Exactly!" Stephanie gave her friend a quick hug. At least Kayla didn't think she was being silly. Even though Kayla was her newest friend, Stephanie often marveled at how alike they thought.

"Let's get back to this sailing thing," Allie said. "I've never been on a boat in my life. What if I get seasick?"

"You'll be fine." Stephanie showed Allie the flyer. "It says it's very safe and we sail only in calm waters."

"And there's no experience necessary," Kayla added. "They teach you everything you need to know. There will be lots of people in the same boat as you." She clapped her hand over her mouth as everyone laughed at her bad joke. "Sorry," she said, giggling.

"Hey!" Darcy grabbed the flyer from Kayla. "We get to participate in a big race, The Marina Regatta. That will be awesome."

"That does sound exciting," Allie agreed.

Anna peered at the flyer. "It says we get to spend a few nights sleeping on the boat. That sounds like fun."

"And don't forget the post-regatta dance," Kayla told her. "Dancing under the stars on a moonlit night," she added dreamily.

Stephanie's eyes lit up. "If that wouldn't be the

most romantic way to meet Mr. Perfect, I don't know what would be!"

*This could be exactly what I'm looking for,* Stephanie thought with excitement. *Mr. Perfect could be waiting for me on that boat!*

Allie was still doubtful. "I'm not sure this is the best way to spend our summer vacation."

Stephanie's father, Danny Tanner, passed by in the hallway, pulling a huge gray rug-cleaning machine behind him.

"Hi, girls," he said, poking his head into the room. "Are you still deciding what to do this summer? Because I have a perfect project for you."

Stephanie raised her eyebrows. "Why am I sure I don't want to hear this?" she asked.

Danny patted the gray machine. "Isn't this a beauty? I just rented it. I'm planning to shampoo all the rugs in the house and then wax all the floors. I might even do the garage. And that's where you all come in."

Stephanie, Darcy, Allie, Kayla, and Anna exchanged a look of dread. Danny was famous for being a neat freak. Cleaning was his favorite hobby!

Danny's eyes glowed. "Washing and waxing floors is a perfect project for five girls with time on their hands."

"Uh, thanks anyway, Dad," Stephanie quickly told him. "But I think we just decided how we're spending our vacation." She glanced at her friends and they nodded back.

"Starting Monday, we'll all be down at the marina," she announced. "Learning to crew at Summer Sail!"

"Yo-ho-ho and a bottle of suntan lotion!" Stephanie sang out.

"And a box of seasick pills," Allie added.

Stephanie, Allie, Darcy, Anna, and Kayla steered their bikes into the yacht club parking lot at the Golden Gate Marina.

On their left the clubhouse gleamed in the sun. It was a large, old-fashioned white building with a wrap-around porch surrounded by beds of bright flowers. A wide green lawn swept past the clubhouse down to the edge of the water.

"Look at all those boats!" Kayla pointed toward the docks that lined the bay. Sailboats of all sizes bobbed alongside the docks in their slips.

Stephanie felt a sudden burst of excitement. "Can you believe we're going to learn how to sail one of those?"

"I can't wait!" Darcy exclaimed. "This really was a great idea, Kayla."

Kayla flushed with pleasure. "Thanks. But we'd better hurry. We don't want to be late for our very first sailing lesson."

They locked their bikes in the bike rack.

"Which boat is ours?" Stephanie asked, eager to get on board.

Kayla frowned. "Oh, no! I forgot to bring that orange flyer. I have no idea."

"We'll have to ask for help." Stephanie scanned the dock. "There's someone." She led the way to the edge of the nearest dock, where a boy kneeled, winding a coil of rope around one tanned arm.

Stephanie cleared her throat. "Excuse me," she said. "Do you know where we go for Summer Sail?"

The boy pushed a lock of straight brown hair off his forehead and laughed. Stephanie guessed he was around fifteen years old. "That's a joke, right?" he asked.

"No." Stephanie frowned. "Why would I be joking?"

The boy got to his feet, still laughing. "Because you're about two inches away from the *Sunshine.*" He pointed his thumb backward over his right shoulder. "That's it."

"Oh!" Stephanie shaded her eyes with one hand and squinted at the boat. The name *Sunshine* was painted across its hull in huge black letters.

*Great. Now this guy thinks I'm a total idiot!* she thought. She felt her cheeks become warm with embarrassment.

"The *Sunshine* is beautiful," Anna murmured.

It was one of the biggest boats at the marina. Its decks were made of glossy reddish brown wood. Its brass railings gleamed. The hull was painted a sparkling white. Two tall masts rose midships and towered against the clear blue sky.

"I'm Ryan Nolan, by the way," the boy introduced himself. "I'm one of the junior instructors at Summer Sail."

"Please tell me we don't have to sail the *Sunshine,*" Allie begged. "It's so *big!*"

"Don't worry," Ryan reassured her. "You'll have plenty of help. You won't even learn to sail on your own until you get to the small boats next month. If you last until next month," he added.

"Why wouldn't we?" Stephanie demanded. "Are you saying we won't be good sailors? Because . . ." The words died away as her eyes widened in shock. She grasped Allie's arm and pulled her away from Ryan.

"What's wrong, Steph?" Allie asked.

Stephanie swallowed hard. Her palms began to sweat. She felt as though someone had punched her in the stomach.

*This is it!* she thought. *This is the feeling Becky was talking about!*

She pointed weakly at the deck of the *Sunshine.* "Allie. Look!" she croaked. "It's him!"

# CHAPTER 3

"It's him—who?" Allie asked.

Stephanie could barely get the words out. "Him! Mr. Perfect. The *one*. This is it, Allie. This is fate!"

Allie turned and spotted a blond, blue-eyed boy on board the *Sunshine*, tying a length of rope.

"Am I crazy, or does he look exactly like Zack from Zack and the Zees?" Stephanie asked.

"You're crazy," Allie replied. "Zack has dark hair, and this guy has very blond hair."

"And blue eyes," Stephanie said in a dreamy voice. "You can see how blue they are, even from here. I think he's better looking than Zack!"

Darcy, Anna, and Kayla rushed up to them. "What's going on?" Darcy demanded.

"Stephanie thinks she sees her dream guy," Allie said.

Stephanie nodded toward the boat. "Up there," she said. "Isn't he amazing?"

"He's cute, I guess," Anna said.

"You guess?" Stephanie stared at her as if she'd lost her mind. "He's only the cutest guy I've ever seen in my entire life! How old do you think he is? Nineteen? Twenty?"

"I hope not. Because that's way too old for you," Allie told her in a calm, no-nonsense voice.

"We're wasting time arguing," Stephanie said. "I've got to meet him! But how?"

Ryan stepped up to her. "No problem," he said. "That's Josh Logan. Everyone at Summer Sail will meet him. He's our senior sailing instructor."

Stephanie jumped. She had forgotten that Ryan was standing right behind her. Her cheeks flushed. "Were you listening to our conversation?" she snapped, trying to cover her embarrassment. She didn't want Ryan overhearing her gush about Mr. Perfect. What if Ryan and Josh were friends and Ryan told him how she felt? Complete humiliation!

"I wasn't listening on purpose," Ryan replied. "Believe me, it's not exactly interesting watching girls get all giggly over a college guy. Big deal, so Josh is eighteen."

"Eighteen?" Stephanie's eyes brightened. She jabbed Allie in the side. "That's not so old!"

"Well, we're *all* getting older just standing here," Ryan said. "Let's get on board."

"Fine." Stephanie climbed up the gangplank that led to the deck of the *Sunshine*. Allie, Darcy, Kayla, and Anna followed. Ryan brought up the rear.

Stephanie paused to smooth her hair away from her face. "Oh, no!" she groaned, and glanced down at her cutoff jean shorts and faded green T-shirt. "I can't believe I'm wearing these grubby clothes."

"The flyer said to dress for hard work," Allie reminded her. "We're all wearing our oldest shorts and tees."

"But I didn't know I was about to meet Mr. Perfect," Stephanie complained.

"I know how you feel," Ryan piped up. "I usually wear a tux myself when I'm sailing." He smacked his hand to his forehead in mock horror. "I can't believe I left it at home on the day I met *you*."

Stephanie raised an eyebrow at him. "Was that a joke? Oh, ha-ha."

Ryan laughed.

"Shhh!" Kayla warned. "Here he comes."

Josh strolled toward them, holding a clipboard in one hand. "Hi," he called. "I'm Josh, senior instructor for Summer Sail. And who are the . . ." he counted. "Five of you?"

He flashed a smile right at Stephanie. She felt her heart lurch. He had the most dazzling smile she'd ever seen.

Stephanie motioned toward her friends. "This is Allie, Darcy, Kayla, and Anna," she said. "And I'm . . . I'm. . . ."

Up close, Josh's eyes were more intensely blue than she had imagined. She felt as though they were hypnotizing her. In fact, her mind was totally blank.

"And I'm . . ." She felt a surge of panic.

"She's Stephanie," Darcy said loudly. "Stephanie Tanner."

Josh grinned. "Hey, I forget my name all the time," he told Stephanie. "That's why everybody calls me . . . um, what do they call me?"

Darcy burst out laughing. Allie, Anna, and Kayla giggled.

*He's not just gorgeous,* she thought. *He's funny, too! I am definitely in love!*

Josh handed them each a blank name tag to fill out. "You'll need to wear these at first," he told them. "We have about thirty kids signed up this month."

Stephanie realized almost that many kids had

gathered on board while they were talking. Josh moved away to hand out their name tags.

"Thirty kids. That's a big group," Kayla said. She smiled at Stephanie. "Maybe the rest of us will meet our perfect guys here, too."

"If we're lucky," Allie remarked in a hopeful voice.

"Luck has nothing to do with it," Stephanie reminded her. "It's fate. Something made Kayla sign us up for this program. And it was fate, I know it!"

"Then, you really think it's fate for you to be here?" Darcy asked.

"Totally," Stephanie replied. "This was meant to be. We're all going to have a completely fantastic summer. And nothing is going to spoil it."

"Oh, no?" Darcy nodded toward the gangplank. "Maybe you'd better check out who's coming."

Stephanie turned her head. "The Flamingoes!"

"What are *they* doing here?" Allie groaned.

Stephanie watched in horror as the four girls strode up the gangplank. Darah Judson led the way. Darah was beautiful. Her masses of long, curly auburn hair bounced around her shoulders as she walked. She was tall and slender, and always wore clothes that showed off her trim figure. Today she wore a bright pink tank top and matching pink shorts. A gleaming white sweatshirt was knotted around her shoulders, setting off her perfect tan.

"This is a disaster!" Stephanie exclaimed.

"I can't believe they signed up for Summer Sail." Kayla shook her head in dismay.

"Is this fate, too?" Darcy commented. "I mean, what are the chances of all of us being here?"

Stephanie didn't answer. She just watched the Flamingoes with increasing dismay.

Darah stopped short as she caught sight of Stephanie. Then she plastered a phony smile across her face and walked right up to her. Tiffany Schroeder, Cynthia Hanson, and Mary Kelly exchanged glances of surprise as they followed Darah across the deck.

"Stephanie!" Darah exclaimed. "I didn't expect to find you and your friends here."

"Believe me, we weren't expecting you, either," Stephanie replied. "Where's Rene?" she asked, scanning the deck for the Flamingoes' pushy leader.

Darah smiled again. "Rene went to Europe with her family," she answered. "She'll be gone the whole summer."

"Really? The whole summer?" Stephanie suddenly felt much better. Rene Salter was the worst of the Flamingoes. It seemed that the Flamingoes' leader had make it her personal mission to make life as miserable as possible for Stephanie and her friends.

*With Rene gone, things are definitely looking up!* Stephanie thought.

Darah's piercing green eyes scanned the group of kids crowding the deck. "Well, this should be fun," she commented.

"Learning to sail is hard work," Stephanie pointed out. *Maybe that will discourage the Flamingoes from signing up,* Stephanie hoped. *They don't like doing anything that might keep them from looking perfect all the time or showing off.*

"Oh, you don't have to tell me that," Darah replied. "We've been sailing for years."

"We love it," Tiffany added. Cynthia and Mary nodded in agreement, broad smiles on their faces.

"But if you already know how to sail, why are you here?" Anna demanded.

*And why are you acting so friendly?* Stephanie wanted to add.

"Why, for the regatta, of course," Darah said. "This is the first year the marina is entering a boat crewed by teens. You've never raced before, but believe me, there is nothing like it."

Stephanie gazed at Darah. The Flamingo seemed genuinely excited by the idea of entering the race. *Could it be true? Could Darah actually be interested in something besides herself and proving how popular she is?*

"We'd better get those silly name tags," Darah

said. "See you." She brushed a stray curl from her face and led her friends away.

"What are they up to?" Darcy asked.

"I hate it when they act friendly," Allie added. "It's almost worse than when they're nasty."

"Yeah, but did you hear the most important thing that Darah said?" Stephanie asked. "Rene is gone—for the whole summer!" She let out a loud whoop.

"You're right. That is important," Allie agreed. "Maybe they won't be so mean with Rene gone."

"They couldn't be," Kayla said. "Darah isn't half as nasty and sneaky as Rene."

"No one is," Anna added.

"And Mary's not so bad sometimes," Darcy said. "We used to play together when we were little. Of course, that was way before she became a Flamingo."

"Tiffany and Cynthia are not my favorite people," Allie admitted. "But they do only what Rene tells them. And with Rene gone . . ."

"I wonder . . ." Stephanie could barely contain her excitement. "Maybe this is part of it, too."

"Part of what?" Anna looked confused. "What are you talking about?"

"Fate!" Stephanie declared. "Maybe fate has taken Rene out of the picture—to make sure I have the perfect summer with my perfect guy! We all will!"

"I don't know," Darcy said uncertainly. "I mean,

you're right—Rene was the worst of them, but with Darah as their new leader, I bet the Flamingoes will be even more popular."

"Yeah," Annie agreed. "Darah is a total boy-magnet. Just look at her."

"Don't look at *her,*" Darcy said. "Look at the guys."

Stephanie glanced around the deck. Darcy was right. The guys were practically falling all over themselves trying to attract Darah's attention. Except for the ones that were playing it super cool. But still, Stephanie could see them sneaking glances at all the Flamingoes.

Darah pretended to be oblivious, but Stephanie knew she was eating it up. She tossed her hair and shot smiles at some of the boys. *Darah looks like a princess acknowledging her loyal subjects,* Stephanie thought. *And all she's doing is going up to Josh to get a bunch of name tags.*

"Oh, no!" Stephanie gasped. "Josh." A terrible thought just occurred to her.

"What's wrong?" Darcy asked.

"Darah will see Josh, and it will all be over." Stephanie moaned.

"Maybe he won't like her," Allie said, trying to look as if she believed it. "Maybe Darah's not his type."

"Are you kidding?" Anna raised her eyebrows.

"Darah is gorgeous. She looks way older than fifteen, too. She's every guy's type."

Stephanie bit her lip. Was Anna right? Was it all over for Stephanie?

She watched with a sinking heart as Josh crossed the deck to the Flamingoes.

Darah glanced up—right into Josh's eyes. He looked startled. Stephanie could hardly bear to listen. But she had to—she had to find out if she still had a chance with Josh.

"Oh. Hi," Darah said. "I'm Darah. I'm here for Summer Sail."

"Uh—I'm Josh. Senior instructor," he replied.

Darah introduced her friends and asked for the name tags. "I wonder why I haven't seen you before?" Stephanie heard Darah ask. "My parents are members of the yacht club. I'm around here a lot."

"I'm new here," Josh explained. "I just finished my first year at San Francisco State."

"Really?" Darah smiled. "Well, I already have a lot of sailing experience," she went on. "So do my friends."

"I think you'll still learn a lot from Summer Sail," Josh said.

"I'm sure." Darah nodded politely—and walked away. Her friends followed.

"I don't believe it!" Stephanie's jaw dropped in amazement. "She didn't even flirt with him."

"This is completely weird," Anna declared.

"It's so spooky, I have the shivers," Kayla said. "There's only one way to explain what just happened."

The others stared at her. "Stephanie must be right," Kayla explained. "It must be her fate to get Josh. How else can you explain the way Darah acted?"

"This is unreal," Stephanie murmured. *Is it true?* she wondered. *Is fate making sure I get Josh and Darah doesn't?*

"Look! Josh is headed this way." Kayla nudged Stephanie with her elbow. "Think fast, Steph. You've got to make him forget he ever even saw Darah. That will clinch it."

"Do something," Allie ordered.

Stephanie gulped. Her friends were right. With the Flamingoes on board, she couldn't be too careful. She had to make sure she made an impression on Josh. But how?

He was headed right toward her. *Do something!* she told herself. She figured she'd think of something to say once she got to him. She quickly smoothed down her hair and took a step in his direction.

Her heart raced as he caught her eye and smiled at her. Then he frowned.

"Watch out!" he shouted.

# CHAPTER 4

◆ ◆ ◆ ◆

*Whaa—?*

Stephanie felt her feet fly out from under her. A bucket clattered down the deck. Before she knew what was happening, she tripped and fell, sprawling onto her stomach. She slid across the deck, stopping a few feet from Josh's feet.

Her cheeks burned with embarrassment as the entire crowd around her burst out laughing. She even noticed Josh's beautiful blue eyes crinkling in merriment.

*Why didn't I slide right off the deck and into the water?* Stephanie thought. *Then I could swim away and never be seen again.*

Darah suddenly appeared, kneeling beside

Stephanie. She gripped Stephanie's elbow to help her up. As they rose from the deck, Darah whispered into her ear, "Have a nice trip?"

Stephanie leaned away from Darah and stared at her.

Darah gazed back coolly, a smug expression on her face. "Is that what they mean by 'kick the bucket'?"

*Darah did this,* Stephanie realized, shaking the Flamingo's hand off her arm. *But why?* Then the answer came to her. *Because she's a Flamingo, silly. That's all the reason Darah needs to be mean.* She had been nice only to keep Stephanie off guard.

"Are you okay?" Josh asked, hurrying over to the two girls.

"She's fine," Darah answered for Stephanie. "But I bet she feels even clumsier than usual."

Stephanie's mouth dropped open at the nasty remark but decided not to respond. "I'm fine," she muttered, keeping her head down so Josh couldn't see her cheeks flaming red.

"Well, be careful," Josh warned her. "Don't want to see you break any of those pretty bones."

Stephanie's head snapped back up. *Did he just say I was pretty?* Stephanie's heart skipped a beat. "I'll try to stay in one piece," she promised with a grin.

"Good," he said. "I've got to get this session

started. See you later." He crossed to a group of older kids carrying clipboards.

Stephanie glanced at Darah to see if she had heard Josh's compliment. Darah had simply stalked away and rejoined the other Flamingoes.

Suddenly Stephanie was surrounded by all her friends. "Are you all right?" Darcy asked.

"Are you hurt?" Allie added. "You really went flying."

"Tell me about it," Stephanie replied. "I'm so embarrassed! And all I wanted to do was make a good impression on Josh."

"Wow, Stephanie," Ryan said, stepping up to the group. "I guess you really fell hard for Josh, huh?" He chuckled.

Stephanie rolled her eyes.

"Get it?" he asked. "Fell hard? You know—"

"I got it the first time," Stephanie said.

"How come you didn't see that bucket?" Ryan pointed to an orange plastic bucket lying on its side near the railing. "Too busy staring at Josh?"

"Where did that bucket come from, anyway?" Darcy asked. "I didn't notice it before."

"There's always stuff lying around on ships," Ryan commented. "You have to stay on your toes."

*Especially when there are Flamingoes aboard,* Stephanie thought.

"Uh-oh," Ryan interrupted. "They're assigning crew groups. Better listen up."

Stephanie glanced up and saw that Josh was now standing on a small raised platform. A sandy-haired guy stood next to him.

"This is Craig Walter," Josh announced. "Craig graduated from college this year—and he was lucky enough to be put in charge of the Summer Sail program."

"Lucky is right." Craig's brown eyes twinkled as he smiled. "Sailing is my life! I hope you'll feel that way, too. Josh and our other instructors are top-notch. Pay attention and learn a lot. Now, tell them about their day, Josh."

Josh nodded. "Each morning we'll meet first thing on the *Sunshine* to read the duty roster—it's a list of your work assignments. Everyone on a boat shares chores. After chores we'll have lessons on deck. We break for lunch, then in the afternoons we take the boat out for hands-on sailing lessons. This is all weather-dependent, of course."

Stephanie couldn't imagine a better way to spend a day than out on the water with Josh. Standing silhouetted against the bright blue sky, he looked like a star in a movie. She loved the way the sea breeze ruffled his hair, which looked positively golden in the sunlight.

Josh gazed out at the group. "You'll be learning

about a lot more than sailing," he promised. "This sport teaches you about teamwork, too. That's one reason we're going to be entering the regatta. There's no better way to learn to work together than by sharing a goal."

Craig nodded. "This race is an important one for the club. We're hosting the event this year and there will be plenty of news coverage. We want all of San Francisco to know about us and be proud of us."

"Not to put any pressure on you or anything," Josh joked.

*We just have to win that race,* Stephanie thought. *That will be so cool.* Who cared about all of San Francisco—Stephanie wanted to make *Josh* proud of her.

"You will be assigned to teams," Craig explained. "Each team will be rotated through the different stations on the ship. That way, by the end of the session—just in time for the regatta—you will have handled each on-board task. Josh, why don't you assign the groups."

Josh read out the list of instructors and crew members. Stephanie crossed her fingers. *Please let me be on Josh's team. Please let me be on Josh's team,* she chanted silently. She glanced around at the other kids. *And please don't let the Flamingoes anywhere near him.*

When the Flamingoes were assigned to Judy's group, Stephanie let out a sigh of relief. *One wish granted,* she thought, *now on to the next.*

To her dismay, instead of being assigned to Josh's crew, she was assigned to Ryan's. "Oh, no," she groaned when Josh called her name. To make matters worse, Kayla, Darcy, Anna, and Allie were together on one crew with another instructor, Fran.

"Why can't I be with you guys?" Stephanie wailed. "This is so unfair."

"Maybe you can switch," Darcy suggested.

"Good idea." She didn't want Josh to think she was some kind of whiny brat trying to get special treatment, though. Besides, he seemed to be involved in a serious discussion with Craig, and she didn't want to interrupt. She spotted Ryan. He seemed like the logical person to ask.

She hurried over. "Listen, I don't mean to cause trouble—"

"Then don't," Ryan cut her off, grinning at her. "Sorry, but whenever someone starts a sentence that way, I get nervous."

Stephanie gave him a quick smile and started over. "I was just wondering if I could be in the same group as my friends." She pointed to Kayla, Anna, Allie, and Darcy, who were gathering around Fran.

"Sorry, no can do," Ryan told her. "We change

one assignment, we'll end up reshuffling everyone. What's the matter? Afraid you'll get lonesome without your buddies? Don't worry, I'll keep you company."

Stephanie rolled her eyes. "Oh, goody," she muttered. She gazed over her shoulder. Josh was still talking to Craig. "What about Josh's team?" she asked.

"Josh doesn't have a team," Ryan explained. "He works with everyone. But I promise that you'll have a good view of Mr. Wonderful from anywhere on the ship."

*Why did he have to overhear me talking about Josh?* Stephanie thought. *I'm never going to hear the end of it!*

*But at least no one is assigned to Josh.* Stephanie figured she had at least as good a chance with him as anyone. As long as she was on the lookout for Flamingoes.

"Stephanie," Ryan interrupted her thoughts. "Did you even hear what I said?"

"Sorry." Stephanie flashed him a smile. "Just thinking how lucky I am to be in your group."

"Yeah, right." Ryan introduced her to the other members of her group. Sam was a short, stocky boy about her own age. Lucy was a pretty brunette about sixteen. She wore gold-wire-rimmed glasses and gave Stephanie a friendly smile.

"First of all," Ryan said, "you should learn correct boating terms. The front of the boat is called the bow. The back end is called the stern. When you're facing the bow, the starboard side is on your right. The port side is on your left."

Stephanie tried to memorize the new terms as Ryan picked up a coil of rope.

"The first thing we'll learn today is how to tie two important knots," Ryan went on. "The bowline and the figure eight. They secure the jib."

Lucy frowned. "What's a jib?"

"See that big sail behind the mast?" Ryan pointed.

"Do you mean the mast that's closer to the front of the boat?" Stephanie asked.

Ryan raised one eyebrow. "You mean close to the *bow* of the boat, don't you, Steph?"

"Huh? Oh, right. Yes, closer to the bow," she repeated.

"Good." Ryan nodded. "That's the mainsail. The smaller sail in the bow is called the jib."

Ryan demonstrated how to make the two knots. Stephanie, Sam, and Lucy carefully studied his movements. Ryan handed them each a length of rope. "Here—try it yourselves," he said.

Stephanie finished her knots quickly while Lucy was still concentrating on her length of rope. Sam made a messy tangle of his piece. "This is impossible," he muttered.

"Here," Stephanie told him. "I think I've figured it out. Watch me."

She helped Sam untangle his rope. Then she showed him how to make a perfect bowline.

"See?" she said, holding it up. "It's easy!"

"Whoa!" Sam's eyes widened in admiration. "That's good."

"That *is* pretty good," Ryan said, looking over her shoulder.

"Why are these knots so important?" Lucy asked.

"Tying a good knot could save your life someday," Ryan explained. "You'll see in a minute, when we take the *Sunshine* for our first cruise."

"We're taking it out? Today? Now?" Sam gaped at Ryan in astonishment. "B-but we don't know anything yet!"

"Don't worry," Ryan reassured him. "The instructors will do all the hard stuff. You guys just have to help out a bit."

Sam looked positively green.

It turned out that Ryan was right—the instructors did the real work. The Summer Sail kids just did what they were told.

Josh, Ryan, and the other instructors yelled commands to one another so fast, Stephanie barely understood what they were saying.

She knew they had to raise the mainsail. And then they adjusted the other sails until they filled with just the right amount of wind.

Then someone lowered the boom, whatever that meant. Then someone else took over tacking—which seemed to have something to do with the way the *Sunshine* turned left and then right as it left the dock to pull into the harbor.

Josh was at the helm, steering. Stephanie watched him as much as she could. He seemed so in command, so sure of himself—it took her breath away.

She also had to pay attention to her own group. They were in charge of some ropes—Ryan kept adjusting them and she and the others had to make sure they were tightly wrapped around big brass holders called cleats. Stephanie could see Ryan had been right—a badly tied knot could cause a lot of trouble.

The sail kept them busier than she expected, but it was more fun than she expected, too.

The *Sunshine* seemed to skim over the top of the water. Salt spray soon covered her face and arms. Under the warm sun it felt wonderful.

"This is incredible! I feel like we're flying!" Stephanie called to Ryan.

"I know! Isn't it great?" Ryan called back.

Stephanie noticed that the instructors were scurrying around the ship again, making new adjustments.

"What are you guys doing now?" Stephanie asked.

"We're turning around so we can head back in," Ryan explained. He waved his team over. "Listen, you guys can take a break. The instructors will handle things from here."

"Great!" Stephanie hoped her friends' group was also told to break. She grabbed a soda from her backpack and went to find them.

She passed the wooden cabin that sat in the middle of the deck. Below the cabin were the kitchen—otherwise known as the galley—and the bunks for their overnight stay. Stephanie barely glanced at the cabin as she headed toward the steering wheel.

Then she stopped dead in her tracks.

Two people stood at the wheel, huddled close together.

One was Josh.

The other, so close to him that she could have been dancing with him, was Darah!

# CHAPTER 5

Stephanie stared in shock.

Josh turned and saw her. He moved away from Darah. "Hey, Stephanie. Want a turn at the helm?" he called in a friendly voice.

Darah gave Stephanie a phony smile. "Oh, that's nice of you, Josh," she said. "But I know how busy you are. I'm sure I could teach the younger kids. I'd be glad to show Stephanie what you just showed me."

Stephanie felt her face flush with anger. "Younger kids!" She fumed. "You're only a year older than I am!"

"Oh, you're right," Darah answered. "I guess you just seem so much younger." She turned to

Josh. "Thanks for the lesson. You explain things so clearly. Bye, Steph." She gave Stephanie another smile before leaving.

"Is something wrong?" Josh asked, noticing Stephanie's flushed face. "You seem upset."

"It's just that my friends and Darah's friends don't exactly get along," she answered.

Josh seemed surprised. "Really? Darah seems so nice."

Stephanie opened her mouth to argue, then shut it again. *Of course,* she realized. *The Flamingoes act friendly in front of Josh. Then, if I complain about them, I look bad!*

"Want a turn?" Josh gestured to the wheel.

Stephanie tried to hide her surprise and nervousness. He was going to trust her at the helm? "Sure. Thanks," Stephanie said. *I hope I don't make a total fool of myself.*

Josh positioned her behind the wheel. Stephanie's pulse raced as he stood behind her. She was hyper-aware of him. He was so close to her that she could smell his coconut-scented sun block.

*Stay calm. Act cool,* she ordered herself. She tried to act as if she were around totally gorgeous college guys every day.

"Stephanie?" Josh said. "Did you hear me?"

"Huh?" Stephanie glanced at him in confusion.

"I was explaining how to adjust the wheel," Josh

said. "Can you steer fifteen degrees to starboard side?"

"Right." Stephanie colored. *How embarrassing!* she thought. *First I go flying at him on my stomach—now I act like a moron who can't understand simple directions!*

Stephanie grasped the heavy wooden wheel and tugged. It was heavier than she expected. To her surprise, she had to really pull hard and concentrate to turn the wheel the right number of degrees.

"This is tough!" she exclaimed.

"That's why steering takes lots of practice," Josh told her. "You should have respect for every one of the jobs on board a boat," he added. "Even things that seem small or silly are important."

Just then, Ted, one of the other instructors, came up to the wheel. He was surrounded by his group of Summer Sail kids. "I thought I'd show my team what's involved in steering," Ted said.

"Great," Josh replied, moving away from the wheel. "Come on, Stephanie, let's take a break."

Stephanie was thrilled. Josh had just invited her to take a break with him. It was practically a date. Then she almost laughed. *Get a grip, Steph,* she scolded herself. *Even* you *aren't crazy enough to think "taking five" counts as a real date.*

Stephanie followed Josh over to a bench by the

railing. He leaned against it and gazed across the bay.

"Have you been sailing a long time?" Stephanie asked as she stood beside him. She wanted to know everything about him.

"I guess I've been sailing my whole life," he told her. "Growing up near the water in San Diego, my family was really into it." He laughed. "I think I swam before I walked."

Stephanie laughed with him. "I love living near the water, too," she said. "But this is the first time I've tried sailing."

"And? How do you rate my favorite pastime?"

"A definite ten." *And on a scale of one to ten,* she added silently, *you rate about one hundred.*

"I'm really glad you're enjoying it," he said.

Stephanie's heart skipped a beat. It seemed to matter to him that she like the same things he did. *A boy cared about that only if he liked you!*

"I never realized how complicated sailing is until I joined Summer Sail," Stephanie confessed. She gave him a big smile. "But you make it look easy."

"It's just practice. But it's always a challenge."

"What do you mean?" Stephanie asked. She was thrilled that he didn't tell her to go rejoin her group, or say that he was busy. He seemed to want to talk to her.

"Sailing is about working *with* nature, not

against it. You have to cooperate with the wind, with the tides, the waves. You know what I mean?"

Stephanie nodded. "I think so." A strong breeze blew her hair into her face and she pushed it aside. "You have to learn to read the signs nature is sending you so you know what to do," she said. "Nature controls the wind, but you control the boat."

Josh gazed at her with admiration. "That's it exactly."

The wind came up again, but this time Josh reached over and brushed Stephanie's hair out of the way. She thought she would faint when he actually tucked it behind her ear and grinned.

"I guess nature is telling you to tie your hair back," he joked.

"Or cut it all off," Stephanie quipped.

"Oh, don't do that," Josh told her. "It looks great just like it is."

Stephanie was glad she had the railing to grab, otherwise she would probably have fallen over. *This is amazing,* she thought. *My knees actually feel weak. I thought that happened only in romance novels.*

Luckily, Josh didn't seem to notice. "It's nice to talk to a new Summer Sail recruit who understands how I feel about sailing," Josh said. "Sometimes the beginning sailors think I'm a little nuts on the subject." He gave Stephanie a warm smile and patted her hand. "I have a good feeling about you, Stephanie."

"And I have a great feeling about Summer Sail," she replied.

"I've hogged too much of your time," Josh said. "You need to get back to your group, and I have to help get the boat ready to dock."

Stephanie wanted to protest, but Josh put his hands on her shoulders and turned her around. "Now scoot," he said in a teasing tone.

"Aye, aye, captain," she joked back. She could hear him laugh behind her as she hurried to find her friends.

*I was totally right,* she thought. *He is my Mr. Perfect. Fate brought us together and nothing is going to keep us apart!*

The following Monday, Stephanie woke early. She couldn't wait to get out to the marina and start sailing. Her entire week at Summer Sail had been complete bliss! Josh always seemed to be around her, giving her pointers on how to improve her sailing skills or telling her jokes to make her laugh.

With each passing day, Stephanie grew more and more certain that Josh was her Mr. Perfect—her destiny guy!

Stephanie dressed quickly and raced downstairs. She poured herself a big bowl of cereal and a glass of orange juice. If there was one thing Stephanie learned from her week on the *Sunshine,* it was that sailing took a lot of energy. She wanted to make sure she was powered up for her long day.

Her dad and her sisters, D.J. and Michelle, were already sitting at the table, munching on toast and eggs. Joey was sleeping late. Uncle Jesse and Aunt Becky had taken the twins out, so the breakfast table was relatively peaceful.

"Hey, Steph!" D.J. smiled. "Dad just told us you're racing in the big regatta this year. Totally cool."

"Yeah," nine-year-old Michelle said. "It's fun to know someone on one of the boats. Then we know who to root for."

"It'll be even more fun to be the one racing!" Stephanie said, her eyes bright with excitement.

"The station wants us to cover the event," Danny Tanner said. Stephanie's father and her aunt Becky were the hosts of a morning television program called *Wake Up, San Francisco.*

"The regatta is a really big deal this year since the marina is hosting it," Danny continued. "There's a lot of media coverage already planned."

"Why so much fuss this year?" D.J. asked, reaching for the milk.

"They alternate host marinas each year," Stephanie explained. "Plus, we're the first crew that's almost entirely made up of beginners. Josh told me that if we place well, the publicity will be great for Summer Sail. It would be even better if we won, of course."

Michelle rolled her eyes. "How many more times is Stephanie going to talk about *Josh?*" she complained. "She's mentioned him only about a gazillion times this week."

"Now, honey, Stephanie's just excited that she made some new friends," Danny said to Michelle. "So no teasing."

*A new gorgeous friend,* Stephanie added silently.

"I *am* surprised that you and your friends turned down my offer to help clean out the garage," Danny added. He smirked as he spread jam on his toast. "But if you change your mind, remember, I'd be happy to let you try the new floor-cleaning machine."

Stephanie and D.J. exchanged a horrified look and shook their heads. "That's okay, Dad," Stephanie said. "I'll pass."

"Well, I'm out of here." D.J. pushed her chair away from the table. D.J. was nineteen and spending the summer working in an office. Stephanie felt sorry for her. She had to be cooped up inside all day while Stephanie spent her days out on the water with the man of her dreams.

"I need to get going, too," Stephanie said. She

dashed back up to her room. She had to make sure she looked perfect. She planned to get to the marina early so that she could spend some more time alone with Josh. She figured that he would also be there before anyone else, getting ready for the session.

Stephanie eyed her crisp yellow cotton shorts and white crop top in the mirror.

*Looking good,* she told herself. She pulled her hair into a loose ponytail over one shoulder. She smiled, remembering how Josh had tucked her hair behind her ear for her. *So romantic. So sweet.* She tied her hair with a yellow-patterned scrunchie and brushed it until it gleamed.

"Ready or not, Josh, here I come," she told her reflection. She grabbed her backpack and raced downstairs. Twenty minutes later she had locked her bicycle to the bike rack and was climbing the gangplank to the *Sunshine.*

"Hey, Stephanie," Ryan's voice rang out. "You're here early!" He pushed his messy brown hair out of his eyes. "Where are all your friends?"

"They'll be here at the regular time," Stephanie replied. "Isn't Josh here yet?"

"Nope." Ryan held up his clipboard. "Looks like it's just you and me."

"Oh, great," Stephanie muttered. *I got up at the crack of dawn to spend time with Ryan? I can't believe this!* she thought.

"You can help me get a head start on the chores," Ryan said, picking up a hose that lay coiled at his feet. He glanced at her. "You're looking awfully nice. A bit too nice for crewing," he commented over his shoulder. He reached down to turn on the hose. "Meeting someone special? Big plans?" He turned around.

And sprayed water all over Stephanie.

Stephanie shrieked. "What are you doing!" she screamed. She held her hands out, trying to block the stream of water.

"I'm sorry! I'm sorry!" Ryan aimed the hose away from her, but the damage was done. She was soaked. Her hair hung down in limp wet strands and her clothes dripped.

"You . . . you . . . !" Stephanie sputtered. She glared at Ryan accusingly.

Ryan laughed. "I'm sorry, I didn't realize the pressure was on so high."

"You're supposed to swab the deck, not the sailors," a deep voice behind Stephanie said.

Stephanie's whole body slumped. She couldn't bear the idea of turning around. She just shut her eyes and wished she could disappear.

She knew that voice. It belonged to Josh. He arrived just in time to see her looking exactly like a drowned rat.

# Chapter 6

All Stephanie could think of was how horrible she must look.

She had wanted to impress Josh, but instead she looked like a total mess.

*And even worse, Josh probably thinks Ryan and I were horsing around like a pair of immature kids. Josh takes sailing so seriously.*

She groaned inwardly as Josh frowned at her. *Uh-oh, here comes the lecture,* she thought. Her mood instantly lightened with his next words.

"You're going to freeze in those wet clothes, Stephanie," Josh said. "I think I have an extra sweatshirt back in my locker. Let's go get it for you."

"Th-thanks," Stephanie stammered. "See you later," she called over her shoulder to Ryan. Ryan seemed a little disgruntled as she followed Josh down the gangplank. He was probably disappointed that he couldn't boss her around anymore that morning, Stephanie figured.

"This is really nice of you," Stephanie told Josh. "To lend me your sweatshirt."

Josh smiled down at her. "Can't have my star pupil catching pneumonia," he said.

She squeezed her hair, trying to get some of the water out of it. "I wish I had a blow dryer," she complained. "And a comb. I must look like a total mess."

"You look just fine to me," Josh assured her.

Stephanie wondered if he noticed that her smile was so broad, it might split her face in two. He was walking close beside her, and occasionally their arms brushed. Every time it happened, Stephanie felt her skin tingle. *I bet we look like a real couple, walking across the lawn together.* She wished her friends were there to see her. *No,* she thought, *I wish the Flamingoes were here to see us.*

"Here we go," Josh said, opening the door for her. "After you, m'lady."

"Why, thank you, kind sir." Stephanie giggled.

"Wait here," he instructed as they walked into the reception area of the marina clubhouse. "I'll just go grab my sweatshirt out of my locker. I'll see if I can rustle up a towel for your hair. Don't go anywhere."

"I'll be right here," she promised. She watched him disappear through the swinging doors marked Employees Only.

Stephanie sighed and glanced out the windows of the clubhouse. She could see the *Sunshine* gleaming on the water. *It really is a beautiful boat,* she thought. She imagined what it would be like to be on it during the regatta. She pictured the marina crowded with picnickers and TV and newspaper reporters. She and Josh would be together at the helm. They would share the joy of victory, sailing across the finish line to the cheers of the crowds onshore.

She was pulled out of her daydream when she spotted Kayla and Darcy heading up the gangplank. It must be almost time for the Summer Sail session to officially begin. *What's taking Josh so long,* she wondered. *How long can it take to grab a sweatshirt out of a locker? Maybe he's trying to find me that towel. Just because I was worried about my hair. That is just the sweet, considerate kind of thing he would do.*

She caught her reflection in one of the windows. She tried to make her hair look *reasonably* okay so that she would look good by the time Josh returned. She noticed most of the kids had arrived and were heading for the ship. *Where is he?* she wondered again.

"Sorry, Steph, I had something I had to take care of," Josh apologized as he dashed through the swinging doors. He tossed her a towel. "Why don't you see if you can mop up a little before putting on the sweatshirt."

"Okay." Stephanie toweled off her bare arms and legs, then dabbed at her shirt and shorts. She rubbed her hair vigorously, hoping she wasn't totally tangling it. "I think that's the best I can do," she told Josh, wadding up the towel and tossing it onto a nearby bench.

"Here you go." Josh held out the hooded sweatshirt so that Stephanie could slip her arms into it. He stood behind her and gently lifted her damp hair out of the collar. "Turn around," he instructed.

Stephanie happily did as she was told. Her heart fluttered as he zipped up the sweatshirt for her. It was huge on her, and to Stephanie it felt like a big, warm hug.

"Now that you're dry," Josh said, "it's time to get back on the water and get soaked by the sea spray!"

Stephanie laughed, and they headed back to the boat. She felt proud and thrilled as she and Josh walked up the gangplank together. It was totally obvious to everyone that she and Josh had been somewhere alone together. She eagerly scanned the crowd on deck. *Yes! There she was. Darah! Fuming by the doors to the cabins.* There was no way she could have missed the late entrance Stephanie and Josh made.

Stephanie couldn't help it. She gave Darah a smug smile, then turned to Josh. "I just noticed, this must be your college sweatshirt." She held it away from her so she could peer down at the lettering.

"One of them," Josh said. "My mom complains that all my wardrobe consists of is college sweatshirts or college T-shirts."

"I'll take good care of this one, I promise." She gave him a little wave and hurried over to her friends.

As soon as she joined them, she asked in a low voice, "Is he gone?"

Darcy glanced past Stephanie and nodded. "Yeah, he went below."

Stephanie grabbed Darcy's hands and let out a squeal. "It was so great!" she exclaimed. "At first it was terrible, and then it was fantastic, and now it's unbelievable!"

Kayla laughed. "I'm sure that sentence made

sense to you, Stephanie, but we have no idea what you're talking about."

Stephanie took a deep breath and then let out a long sigh. She shook her head. "I'll tell you everything later. When there aren't so many people around."

"Well, you should see Darah's face," Allie said. "She turned every shade of pink there is."

"Yeah, she even turned colors I didn't know existed!" Annie added.

"Good," Stephanie declared. "Now maybe she knows that Josh likes me and she'll keep her hands off."

"I wouldn't count on it," Darcy warned. "There are too many Flamingoes aboard to let your guard down. Besides, has a Flamingo ever let a little thing like a girlfriend stand between her and a boy?"

"Okay, Stephanie, spill it all," Darcy demanded. "And I don't mean your lunch!"

Stephanie laughed. She and her friends were on lunch break in the galley belowdecks. Because the water was choppy, Josh decided to have lessons in the morning with the *Sunshine* docked. He promised they would try to take the boat out in the afternoon. "You always have to take your cues from the weather, not the other way around," he told them.

Still, Stephanie had to admit, if she had to be in class, she couldn't think of a better place than the *Sunshine.* Ryan had taken the group over every inch of the boat, teaching them the names and functions of all the equipment. She was sure she would never be able to keep it all straight.

"Yeah, Stephanie," Kayla urged. "How's it going with you and Josh?"

"It's going great." She told them about the incident with Ryan and the hose and how she came to be wearing Josh's sweatshirt. "Don't you think it means he thinks we could be a couple?" she asked her friends. "Girls borrow their boyfriends' clothes all the time, right?"

Kayla looked thoughtful. "It *could* mean he likes you as a girlfriend," she began to say.

"Or it could mean you were cold and he's a nice guy," Anna pointed out.

"But you didn't hear how he flirted with me," Stephanie protested. She slumped in her seat and shoved her hands into Josh's sweatshirt pockets. Her fingers felt something in one of them. She pulled out an envelope. "What's this?" She turned the envelope over. The letter *S* was scrawled across it.

Stephanie held the envelope out to show her friends. "Look," she said. "It's addressed to *S* That's me! Stephanie."

She flipped the envelope over and opened it. "This must be what took him so long in the locker room," she said. "Now I understand—he was writing this note to me."

As Stephanie scanned the brief note, she felt her face heat up.

"What does it say?" Darcy demanded.

"It must be a love letter," Allie teased. "Look how red her face is."

"Is it, Steph?" Kayla asked. "Is it a love letter?"

"Not exactly," Stephanie admitted. "But it is definitely a 'like' letter."

"Quit torturing us and read the note!" Darcy said.

" 'I'm sorry my Summer Sail responsibilities keep me from spending more time with you,' " Stephanie read, her voice quivering. " 'But I promise I like you as much as sailing—and you know how I feel about sailing!' " She gazed at her friends. "Then there's this little heart next to where he signed his name." She sighed and stared back down at the note. "Isn't that the cutest, sweetest thing you ever heard in your whole life?"

"I'll tell you one thing," Kayla said. "This definitely means he likes you."

*It's really happening,* Stephanie thought in amazement. *My perfect guy thinks I'm his perfect girl.*

What a perfect summer!

# CHAPTER 7

"Read it again," Kayla urged Stephanie.

"No, let me read it," Darcy said, snatching the note away from Stephanie. "My darling Stephanie," she began in a deep, dramatic voice. She glanced up and grinned. "See, I'm reading the parts that he was too shy to put in the note."

"Perfect," Allie said, giggling. "Keep going."

Darcy cleared her throat and continued. "I am so sorry that my Summer Sail responsibilities keep me from spending more time with you, but I am especially sorry that it means I have to put up with those stupid Flamingoes. Especially that horrible Darah. How could she ever think I would like her more than you, when it is so obvious that you are by far the most perfect girl in the whole world."

"Cut it out," Stephanie tried to say, but she was laughing too hard.

"So tell us, Stephanie, how *does* he feel about sailing?" Kayla teased.

"Let me put it this way," Stephanie replied, grabbing the note back from Darcy. "If he likes me even half as much as he likes sailing, I'd be thrilled."

"And he says right here in black and white"—Anna pointed to the note—"that he likes you and sailing equally."

"Your next job is to get him to like you even *more* than sailing," Allie said.

Stephanie laughed. "I think that might be mission impossible."

Darcy nudged Stephanie. "You know, Darah has been watching us this whole time."

Stephanie glanced over at Darah's table. "Good," she said. "Let her watch all she wants."

"Let who watch what?" Josh asked.

Stephanie nearly jumped out of her seat. She hadn't noticed him come up behind her. None of them did. She quickly shoved the note and the envelope back into the sweatshirt pocket. She didn't want Josh to know that she had shown such a personal note to her friends.

"Uh, we all have to watch . . . ourselves . . . so . . . uh . . . so we don't wind up going overboard," Stephanie said. *Way to go, Steph. Boy, did that sound lame.*

"Actually," Josh said with a grin. "At some point you're all going to go overboard."

"What?" Allie asked. "Are we that bad as sailors?"

"Mind if I slip in here, Steph?" Before waiting for her to answer, Josh sat down beside her. Stephanie tried to keep breathing normally. It was a tight fit, and she had to fight to keep from leaning her head against his shoulder.

"What do you mean about going overboard?" Kayla asked.

"Everyone aboard ship should know what to do in case of an emergency. So we'll do some drilling. If you sign up for later sessions," Josh explained, "you'll even capsize your boats on purpose to learn how to right them in the water."

Then he ruffled Stephanie's hair. "I promise to give you advance warning, Stephanie. That way getting soaked won't take you by surprise."

Stephanie giggled. "Thanks. I'll be sure to bring my waterproof hair that day."

Josh laughed, then his face grew concerned. "Are you okay?" he asked. "I mean, are you feeling seasick or anything?"

"What? Why?" Then Stephanie noticed he was glancing down at her uneaten sandwich. "Oh," she explained. "I'm just not very hungry."

He raised an eyebrow. "Oh, yeah? Then I guess you won't mind if I do this." He picked up her sandwich and took a huge bite out of it. He stood, and still chewing, waved good-bye and left the dining hall.

Kayla's eyes were wide as she gazed at Stephanie across the table. "That guy really likes you."

"You think so?" Stephanie's voice came out as a little squeak.

"I mean *really* likes you," Kayla assured her.

"*Really* likes me?"

"Really really *really* likes you," Darcy said, laughing.

*"Really?"*

The whole table cracked up. Stephanie was laughing so hard that she had to wipe the tears from her eyes. When she glanced up again, Darah was standing by her table.

"What are you all so hysterical about?" she demanded.

"We're not hysterical," Stephanie replied. "We're . . . happy."

"Fine. So what are you so happy about, then?" Darah persisted.

"Why should you care?" Darcy asked. "And why should we tell you?"

"No, it's okay, Darcy." Stephanie couldn't wait to see how this news hit Darah. She pulled the envelope out of her pocket and lay it on the table, the *S* faceup. "My friends are happy for me because Josh let me know just how he feels about me." She patted the envelope. "I'd read you the note he sent me, but it's a little too personal."

Darah narrowed her blue eyes. She looked down at the envelope and then back at Stephanie. "Well, I don't know what Josh may have said in that note," Darah said. "But you obviously misinterpreted it."

"No way," Darcy said. "We read the note, and there is no mistaking the message."

"So why don't you Flamingoes go fly away," Stephanie said.

Darah put her hands on her hips and glared down at Stephanie. "Pay attention, Stephanie, because I want to say this only once," she declared. "I don't care what that silly note says. Just stay away from Josh. And if you're hoping he'll ask you out, you're wasting your time. Because he already asked *me* out on a date."

# CHAPTER 8

◆ ◂ ▪ ◆

Stephanie gaped at Darah as she and her fellow Flamingoes flounced away. She was so stunned, she couldn't think of a single thing to say in reply.

"Forget her," Kayla said. "She's probably just making it up."

"Do you think so?" Stephanie asked, biting her lip.

Anna patted her hand sympathetically. "If he asked Darah out, he's not the guy for you anyway."

Stephanie yanked her hand away. She grabbed the envelope and shoved it back into her pocket. "But he *is,*" she insisted. "Maybe Darah forced him into it. Or maybe she's just plain lying, like Kayla said."

"Well, there's only one way to find out," Darcy commented. "Go directly to the source."

"Ask Josh?" Stephanie said. "Just come out and ask him?"

Darcy shrugged.

"That would be so embarrassing. What if it's true?" Stephanie shuddered, thinking about how terrible it would feel to hear Josh say that he preferred Darah after all.

"It's the only way to know for sure," Anna said. "You're definitely not going to get the truth from Darah."

Stephanie sighed. "You're right. I'll ask him as soon as I get a chance to be alone with him. And as soon as I get up the nerve."

"Morning, Steph!" Ryan called as Stephanie strode onto the *Sunshine* the next Monday. She had arrived early, hoping to have a chance to talk to Josh alone.

The past week had been great, but the weekend had been a dismal disaster. All Stephanie could do was imagine Darah and Josh together. Her friends tried to cheer her up, but nothing worked. She moped around her room, playing her Zack and the Zees CDs over and over. Finally on Sunday night she got some good news. Allie and Kayla spotted Darah and the rest of the Flamingoes at the mall

Friday *and* Saturday night. Which meant Darah and Josh didn't have a date that weekend. There was still hope for Stephanie!

Stephanie figured this was proof that Darah must have lied about the date. It was just the confidence booster she needed. She would march up to Josh and find out if he had asked Darah out.

But now that she was back on board she was feeling a few flutters of nerves. *Just get it over with,* she ordered herself.

"Hi, Ryan." Stephanie stood on tiptoe and peered over Ryan's shoulder.

"Looking for somebody?" Ryan asked. "As if I didn't know."

Stephanie frowned. Ryan didn't have to tease her about Josh all the time. "I'm just looking to see if Sam and Lucy are here yet," she told him.

"Right." Ryan shook his head. Clearly, he didn't believe her.

"Morning, everybody!" Josh bounded onto the deck, holding his clipboard. His hair glinted in the early morning sunlight.

Stephanie screwed up her courage. *Just go over there and ask to speak with him privately.* She took a deep breath.

It was too late. The Summer Sail kids were swarming onto the deck. Josh was instantly surrounded by instructors and kids needing his attention.

*You blew it,* Stephanie scolded herself. *Well, the day just started. Keep your eye out for an opportunity to be alone with Josh. And,* she reminded herself with a smile, *at least you know that Josh did not have a date with Darah over the weekend. Everything could still be just fine.* She waved at her friends as they hurried up the gangplank and then she went to join her team.

Ryan was reading over the duty roster with Sam and Lucy. Stephanie's job was to help Lucy remove the covers from the sails. When they were done, Sam handed them mops and buckets. This time the three of them had to swab the entire deck.

When morning chores were done, Craig came on board to give them all a lesson in racing techniques, psyching them up for the big regatta. Stephanie thought racing sounded great—if they could learn enough in time! They broke for lunch, then assembled on deck afterward to get ready for their afternoon sail.

"The regatta is getting closer," Josh reminded them all. "I want all your skills to be in top form by then. You are going to be taking on greater responsibilities each time we go out." He smiled broadly. "That means you're going to be doing more of the real sailing. Which is a lot more fun than chores!"

Everyone on deck laughed.

"Let's get to it, crew!" Josh shouted. All the teams cheered and then sprang into action. The *Sunshine* was alive with activity as the instructors and the students got the boat under way.

"Wow! This is fantastic!" Stephanie stood with her legs braced on the broad deck. She lifted her face into the wind as the *Sunshine* skimmed along the choppy waves at the entrance to the harbor. She let out the line she held in both hands. "How's this?" she asked.

"Great. You're really getting the hang of it, Stephanie," Ryan told her. "You eased out the mainsail just until it started to luff, or flap. Now tighten the line until . . . that's it." Ryan grinned. "You seem to catch on faster than normal people."

"Are you saying I'm not normal?" Stephanie teased.

Josh came up behind them. "Great job with the sails, Stephanie," he said. "Hey, want to try your hand at the wheel again?"

Stephanie felt her heart flutter with excitement. Josh was trying to find a way for them to be together! And this would be her chance to ask him about Darah.

But Ryan frowned. "Um . . . can you do that

tomorrow, Josh?" he asked. "Stephanie needs more pointers on handling the mainsail. After all, she's been in charge of it only once."

Josh nodded. "Whatever you say," he told Ryan. He turned and made his way to the other side of the boat.

"Why did you do that?" Stephanie blurted out as Josh left.

Ryan looked surprised. "You need a few pointers. Don't worry," he added. "You'll have another chance at steering later . . . or should I say another chance at Josh."

Stephanie fumed. She couldn't believe he was teasing her this way—especially in front of Sam and Lucy.

She secured the rope she was holding. "Don't you think Sam and Lucy deserve a turn?" she asked sweetly. Then she turned and stormed off after Josh.

"I didn't give you permission to leave!" Ryan called after her.

"I gave *myself* permission," she shot back.

She found Josh up at the wheel. "Hey, Josh," she said. "I'd love to try steering again if that's okay."

He gave her a big smile and moved aside. She felt a thrill as she stepped up to the heavy wooden wheel.

"Just wait until we come about again," he instructed. "You remember, that means to turn into the wind . . ." he began to explain.

"I know! And the bottom part of the mainsail swings across the boat," Stephanie finished. "And everybody ducks, right?"

"The *what* swings across?" Josh eyed her.

Stephanie groaned. "Oh. The *boom* swings across," she said, using the proper term.

"That's better," Josh commented. "I don't mean to sound like a kindergarten teacher, but its important to use the right terms." He grinned at her. "I mean, we'd sound pretty silly calling out orders like 'now move the thingy there over to the whatchamacallit.' "

Stephanie nodded. "I get your point."

Josh reached past her so he could grab on to the wheel. He made a tiny adjustment. His face practically brushed hers as he peered across the bow of the ship. Stephanie tried not to move an inch. It felt so great to be this close to him.

He stood just slightly behind her, his arms on either side of her. She thought she could stand that way forever. He was practically hugging her. *I have to ask him now,* Stephanie realized. *I won't have a better opportunity. I need to know if he really asked out that Flamingo.*

"Uh, Josh?" she said. But a voice behind them interrupted her.

"Mind if I watch?" Ryan appeared, tucking his brown hair into a cap. "I want to see how my star pupil is doing."

*I was doing fine until you showed up,* Stephanie thought, glaring at him.

"Sure thing," Josh told him.

*Ryan did this on purpose,* she realized. *He knew I wanted to be alone with Josh, so he had to ruin it.*

Josh took a tiny step away from Stephanie, then turned toward her. "Okay," he said. "This is kind of tricky. You need to position the boat at a right angle to the wind. Then try to steer as straight a line as possible until we're clear of all the other boats in the harbor."

Stephanie had to concentrate hard on what she was doing. The *Sunshine* was quick to respond to the wheel. It was hard work to keep it on course. One time, an extra-heavy gust of wind puffed into the sails and the boat veered to the starboard side.

"Whoa!" Josh stepped next to her, wrapping his arms around her shoulders. His strong hands grasped the wheel next to hers. "You could use a little help," he said.

"Yeah," Stephanie choked out. Her heart pounded. She was a bit embarrassed that Josh had to help—but even more thrown by standing so close to him.

*Keep your mind on steering,* she lectured herself.

It was easier said than done. She kept staring at his hands and forearms. He was so tan, and his muscles looked so strong as they twisted the wheel. He wore the cutest little woven good-luck bracelet that had completely faded from the sun and saltwater.

"Okay, back on course," Josh said.

"Why don't you show her how to tack?" Ryan suggested.

"I'm having enough trouble doing this," Stephanie commented.

Ryan shrugged, but Josh was nodding in agreement. "You should learn how to tack," he said. "You tack—or come about—when you change the boat's course by turning *into* the wind. It's tricky, too. But don't worry—you're up to it."

"If you really think so," Stephanie said uncertainly. She wanted so much to impress him. Josh showed her what to do, and Stephanie gave it a try. The *Sunshine* seemed to wobble on top of the water as the wind dropped from the sails.

"Watch it!" Josh cried. He grabbed the wheel again. "Here," he said. "I'd better show you how it's done. Be sure to duck when I swing the boom across.

"Uh-huh." Stephanie nodded and stepped back. Ryan shot her an amused look.

*He's glad I couldn't do it!* she thought. *He wants me to be humiliated in front of Josh! He is such a baby!*

She turned away from Ryan and gazed at Josh as he took command of the wheel again.

Josh was terrific—so patient and sweet. *Not a bit like Ryan,* Stephanie thought. *And Josh wouldn't make fun of me just because I couldn't get it right the first time. Now, if Ryan would just go away, I could finally talk to Josh privately.*

"Hey, Josh." Darah suddenly appeared and Stephanie's heart sank. "Can I give it a shot?"

*Great,* Stephanie thought. *I can just forget about talking to Josh now.*

"Sure, Darah." Josh stepped away from the wheel to give Darah a chance.

Stephanie couldn't stand there watching Darah show off how good she was at steering. She gave up.

"I'm going to find my friends," Stephanie told the others, heading away from the helm. Suddenly the boat lurched as it abruptly shifted directions.

"Steph! Look out!" Ryan's shout rang out through the air. *"Duck!"*

Stephanie whirled around, her eyes wide as she saw the heavy mainsail swing free. The enormous wooden boom was swinging sideways—and was about to smack her in the face!

# CHAPTER 9

Stephanie's breath was knocked out of her as Ryan hurled himself at her. They landed on the deck with a thud. The boom swept over them, missing them by inches.

"What is wrong with you?" Ryan hollered at her. He scrambled to his feet. "Why weren't you paying attention?"

Stephanie felt a little dazed as she gazed up at him. She slowly brought herself to a sitting position.

"Are you all right?" Josh hurried over to her and held out a hand. She took it and he pulled her to her feet.

"Don't you know you have to be alert at all

times?" Ryan demanded. "You could have been badly hurt."

"I'm okay," Stephanie replied. She had never seen Ryan so angry.

Josh glanced at Ryan. "Listen, Ryan, I can take things from here. Why don't you check on the rest of your team?"

Ryan shook his head in frustration at Stephanie. Then he spun on his heel and stalked off.

"I—I don't know what happened," Stephanie began to explain to Josh. She felt the *Sunshine* slowly change direction. Then Darah rushed over.

"Oh, Stephanie, are you all right?" Darah asked, her voice full of concern.

"I'm fine," Stephanie replied.

"I am so sorry," Darah went on. "I don't know how I could have made such a dumb mistake. It is totally my fault, Josh." Darah laid a hand on Josh's arm. "Don't blame little Stephanie, here."

*Little Stephanie?* Stephanie fumed. *What nerve!* She noticed Darah still hadn't let go of Josh's arm.

"I feel just terrible about this," Darah continued. "I didn't think the boat would be so responsive."

"You also forgot to shout 'coming about,'" Stephanie pointed out. She hoped Josh could see through Darah's act.

"I know, I know," Darah moaned. "Please don't

be angry with me, Stephanie. I mean, it's not like I did it on purpose."

*Yeah, right,* Stephanie thought. *And if you think I believe that, you're even dumber than I thought.*

"Accidents happen," Josh said. "I'm sure Stephanie doesn't blame you. But it is a good reminder that we all have to be on our toes on the boat. And during the regatta, things will be happening much faster."

"Don't worry, Josh," Darah reassured him with a dazzling smile. "This won't happen again."

*You can bet on that,* Stephanie vowed silently.

Josh looked at her. "You're awfully quiet, Stephanie," he said. "Are you sure you're all right?"

Stephanie nodded. "I just had the wind knocked out of me."

"Come on, let's go below. You could probably use a soda or something."

Stephanie shot Darah a smug look and then followed Josh belowdecks. She sat at a small table while he rummaged through a mini-refrigerator. He pulled out two cans and handed one to Stephanie.

"Now, you're sure you're okay?" he asked her, leaning against a counter.

"Yeah. More embarrassed than anything else."

"I guess Darah must be pretty embarrassed, herself," he commented.

"Uh, yeah, Darah." Stephanie took a sip of soda. *There's your opening, Steph. Ask him about Darah right now,* she urged herself. "Hey, listen, I heard something, and I just wanted to know if it was true."

He smiled at her. "Okay, I confess, the rumors are true. I'm obsessed with winning the regatta."

She laughed. "That's not it. But that's good to know. No pressure there."

"So what did you want to ask me?" He sat at the table across from her. His eyes seemed even bluer than usual, Stephanie thought. It must be the faded denim workshirt with the torn sleeves that he was wearing. It brought out the color of his eyes.

*Snap out of it and start talking,* Stephanie ordered herself. *Before ten million people interrupt you again.*

She took a deep breath and tried to sound as casual as possible. "I heard that you asked Darah out."

He looked surprised. He pushed the chair away from the table and tipped it onto the back two legs. "Darah? No way." He brought the chair back down with a thud. He smiled broadly at Stephanie, and a faraway look came into his eyes. "There's only one girl for me."

Stephanie glanced down at her lap, the intensity of his gaze was almost too much for her. *Ask him about the note,* she ordered herself. *Tell him you feel the same way about him. Get him to ask you on a real honest-to-goodness date!*

She brought her face back up and noticed Ted dashing down the stairs. Her heart flopped down into her shoes. Their perfect moment alone was over.

"Josh, we're having a little trouble with the mainsail," Ted said. "It's no biggie, but I thought it would be best if you were there."

"Got it." Josh took one last swig of his soda, then pitched the can into the wastebasket. "See you later, Stephanie."

*Well, he may not have asked me out,* Stephanie thought, a huge grin spreading across her face, *but he sure didn't ask Darah out. Just as I figured—Darah was lying the whole time.*

Then Stephanie stopped dead still as a sudden realization hit her. Josh just said he was a one-girl type of guy!

*And that one girl must be me!*

Stephanie hurried across the marina lawn to meet her friends. The instructors decided to dock the *Sunshine* for lunch, and everyone from Summer Sail was scattered around at picnic tables or on the lawn.

"Hi," Allie greeted her. She took a bite of her sandwich and then took a closer look at Stephanie. "You're in a good mood."

Stephanie took her apple and yogurt out of her sack. "I am in a great mood," she declared.

"Let me guess," Kayla teased. "Could it have something to do with one of the sailing instructors?"

Stephanie nodded and peeled back the top of the yogurt container. "I don't think it could go any better," Stephanie said.

"So, has he asked you out?" Anna demanded.

Stephanie shrugged. "Well, no," she admitted. "But I'm not all that worried. I'm sure he will when he gets the chance."

Darcy plopped down beside her on the bench. Her dark eyes sparkled. "Well, he's going to get the chance Thursday," she announced.

"What do you mean?" Stephanie asked, turning to look at Darcy.

"What I mean is, I just came from Craig's office." Darcy jerked her head in the direction of the marina clubhouse. "While I was there I happened to see the special duty roster on Craig's desk. It showed the schedule for our first sleepovers on the boat. Josh was listed for Thursday night," she said. "And so was your group!"

"What? Really?" Stephanie couldn't believe it was true.

"Believe it," Darcy told her. "Your group is staying on the boat the same night as Josh."

Stephanie's eyes widened as she gazed around

her group of friends. "Isn't this the final proof? Josh and I are fated to be together!" Then she thought of something. "What about the Flamingoes?" she asked Darcy. "Please tell me they aren't scheduled for the same night."

"They aren't scheduled for the same night."

Stephanie squealed in delight. "Oh, this is going to be so great!" she gushed. *On the boat with Josh for a romantic night sail. Surely he'd find a chance to get her alone and ask her for a date.*

Maybe he'd even kiss her!

"Unfortunately, it's two groups per overnight," Darcy complained. "And guess who's scheduled for the very first overnight on Tuesday with the Flamingoes."

The rest of the girls at the table let out groans. "That's right," Darcy confirmed. "Us."

After they finished lunch, everyone returned to the boat. The rest of the afternoon was spent learning some of the special conditions that might come up during the regatta. By the time Stephanie saw Josh again, it was right before Summer Sail ended for the day.

"Josh!" she cried in excitement. "I heard you've been assigned to Thursday night with my group. Should I bring anything special?"

Josh frowned. "Actually, I was thinking of changing my night," he told her. "I had something else planned for Thursday. I need to clear it with Craig first, but I'm going to sign up for the first overnight tomorrow night, Tuesday, instead."

"Tuesday?" Stephanie cried in horror. Tuesday was the Flamingoes' night! "B-but—then you won't be supervising my group. You'll be with . . ." She couldn't bear to mention the Flamingoes.

"Well, why not trade nights?" Josh asked.

"Really?" Stephanie stared at him. "Are you sure you wouldn't mind?" she asked.

"Why should I?" Josh grinned. "I know most of your friends are scheduled on Tuesday night already. You'd probably have more fun on the overnight with them."

"Thanks! I will," Stephanie told him.

"Just make sure you find a group to trade with your group, since we have to keep the same numbers each night," Josh told him. "But I'm sure you'll be able to find a group."

*And I know exactly who to ask,* Stephanie thought. *But how will I ever get Darah and the Flamingoes to trade with me?* she wondered.

Stephanie arrived early again on Tuesday. She still hadn't figured out a way to get Darah to switch with her. No matter how hard she racked her brain, no answer came to her.

She bent down to lock up her bicycle, when she heard a voice above her.

"Just the person I wanted to see."

Stephanie glanced up to discover Darah standing over her.

"Why would you want to see me?" Stephanie demanded. "Have another little trick to play?"

Darah brushed her auburn curls from her face and sighed. "That's exactly what I wanted to talk to you about. I think we should have a truce. After all, we don't want to look silly fighting in front of everyone."

Stephanie blinked in surprise. *A truce? With you? In about a million years!* she thought.

"So, I came up with a little peace offering," Darah continued. "I'm sure you're looking forward to spending your night on board the *Sunshine,* right?"

"So?" Stephanie said warily.

"Did you check the duty roster for the sleepovers today?" Darah asked.

"No," Stephanie told her. She hadn't checked it, since she already knew that Josh was changing his night from Thursday to Tuesday. Was Darah going to taunt her with the fact that Josh had switched to Tuesday night—the night the Flamingoes were assigned?

Darah raked her hair away from her face. "Well,

I thought that as proof that I want to end our childish fighting, I would offer to trade nights with you."

Stephanie frowned in confusion. "I don't understand."

"Well, your group is scheduled for Thursday, but all your friends are in a group scheduled for tonight, my group's night. I figured you would rather spend the overnight with them."

Stephanie gaped at her in astonishment. Then she realized what was going on.

The duty list for the sleepover had just been posted that morning. Craig must have left Josh's name in the Thursday night spot. Darah didn't know that Josh wanted to work Tuesday instead.

Darah was trying to make Stephanie trade nights. She thought she would have Josh to herself on Thursday!

*This is too good to be true,* Stephanie realized. She tried to keep her face blank so that Darah wouldn't suspect that Stephanie knew exactly what she was up to.

"Why are you being so nice?" Stephanie demanded, hoping she sounded suspicious enough.

"I told you, it's a peace offering," Darah said, acting hurt.

"Well . . ." Stephanie made herself look doubtful. "It's not totally up to me. I'll have to make sure the rest of my group will want to switch. We are a team, after all."

Stephanie tried not to laugh when she saw the look of annoyance on Darah's face. But the Flamingo tried to cover it with a big, fake smile. "Of course," she said sweetly. "Just let me know as soon as you can." She turned and walked up the gangplank.

Stephanie waited until Darah was out of sight before she let herself burst out laughing. She noticed most of the Summer Sail kids had arrived. She glanced around and waved her friends over.

"What's going on?" Kayla asked.

"Were you just talking to Darah?" Darcy demanded.

"You won't believe it," Stephanie said, trying to control her laughter. "Darah practically begged me to switch nights with her!" She quickly explained about Josh and the duty roster and how Darah didn't realize that Josh wasn't going to be assigned on Thursday night after all.

Darcy hooted with laughter. "You have to be kidding," she declared. "Darah traded *away* her night with Josh?"

"Exactly!" Stephanie replied.

"And it was her own fault." Kayla's eyes danced with amusement. "I love it!"

"She'll be totally steamed when she finds out what she's done," Allie warned.

"Who cares?" Stephanie said. "By then it will be too late."

*For once,* Stephanie thought with satisfaction, *the Flamingoes have outsmarted themselves!*

# CHAPTER 10

"What are you doing, Stephanie?" Kayla held the door to Stephanie's bedroom wide open and gaped.

It was the night of the first overnight of Summer Sail. Allie, Darcy, and Anna crowded around Kayla. Stephanie stood surrounded by an enormous pile of clothes.

"I can't decide what to wear," Stephanie groaned.

"What's wrong with what you have on?" Allie asked.

Stephanie glanced down at her outfit: snug black jeans and a pale blue tank top with a loose black overshirt knotted at the waist.

"It's so—black and blue!" Stephanie wailed.

Kayla laughed. "You have first-date jitters, Stephanie," she said. "That outfit is really cool."

"You think so?" Stephanie asked. "I don't look like I'm trying too hard? After all, we usually wear just shorts and tees."

Anna flopped down on Stephanie's bed. Her usual armful of bracelets jangled as she moved. Anna wore a faded print short-sleeved blouse over a green T-shirt. She also had on a pair of loose-fitting green pants, and her dark hair was swept back from her face and tied with a red scarf.

"Your outfit is so—so *you*," Stephanie told her. "Why can't I wear something like that?"

"Because you're not Anna," Allie pointed out. "Relax, Steph. You look great."

"Besides," Darcy added, "you know Josh by now. He doesn't seem to notice what any of us are wearing."

"Darcy's right," Anna said. She glanced at her watch. "It's getting late. Aren't we supposed to be at the marina by seven?"

"Yeah, but we have a few minutes more," Stephanie answered.

"You're lucky the rest of your group didn't mind trading," Anna commented.

"I figured they wouldn't care," Stephanie explained. "They're all so good-natured, they'd agree to almost anything."

"Well, we're grateful because it means our group doesn't have to deal with the Flamingoes," Kayla said.

Stephanie grabbed her overnight bag and her backpack. Her dad was driving them all to the marina.

Ten minutes later Danny pulled into the marina parking lot. The five girls climbed out and slammed the car doors. Danny got out too. He stared at the *Sunshine* rocking gently in its slip.

"Are you sure you'll be okay, staying out here all night?" he asked, concerned.

"Dad, we went over this a hundred times," Stephanie told him. "We'll be very closely supervised. Our instructors have a lot of experience. They know exactly what they're doing. Nothing could possibly go wrong."

"Thanks for the compliment, Stephanie," a voice said. "I think it's the first nice thing you've said about me all summer."

Stephanie whirled around. To her dismay, she found herself face-to-face with Ryan. "What are *you* doing here?" she asked.

"I'm that experienced instructor you just described to your dad," Ryan said. "At your service!"

"Will you be the only instructor on board?" Danny asked.

"No way," Ryan answered. "Jenny's coming, too, and maybe even Fran. I could never handle this mob on my own!"

"Wait," Stephanie said. "What about Josh? You didn't mention Josh."

"Josh is scheduled for Thursday night," Ryan answered.

"He *was,*" Stephanie told him. "But he switched to tonight. He told me."

Ryan shrugged. "That's the first I've heard of it. I'm pretty sure Josh said he had someplace special to go tonight."

Stephanie stared, dumbfounded. Ryan picked up his duffel bag and headed for the docks.

"Ryan seems like a responsible kid. But I hope the other instructors are older," Danny said.

"They are," Stephanie replied, staring after Ryan in shock.

*How did this happen?* she wondered. *I know Josh wanted to be here tonight. He said so. Something had happened to change his mind. But what?*

Danny waved good-bye and pulled out of the parking lot.

"Tough break, Steph," Allie told her.

"Yeah. I'm really sorry," Darcy added. "But look

on the bright side. At least there aren't any Flamingoes around."

"That's true," Stephanie mumbled. She was so disappointed. She followed Darcy as they climbed onto the *Sunshine*. They stowed their gear down below, in the girls' cabin.

As they hurried back on deck, they found Ryan talking to the rest of the group—Sam and Lucy from Stephanie's group and Andrew, Dave, and Rob from Jenny's group. Not everyone could make it. There were ten kids and three instructors in all.

"We won't really sail tonight," Ryan said. "We'll cruise the harbor with the motor on. We plan to stay out until after dark. Nighttime sailing is different from what you're used to."

"That's right," Fran went on. "For one thing, we'll need to use our lights, so other boats can see us. The red sidelight shows which is our port side, and the green shows our starboard."

"Our mastlight tells everybody when we're riding with the motor on," Jenny said, pointing to a fixed white light attached high up on the mast. "The other boats know the signals—it's a special sailing language. This will give you all a chance to learn new navigating techniques."

"And we might even have *some* fun, too," Ryan added with a chuckle.

Jenny went to the engine room, and a few minutes later Stephanie heard the motor start to chug. She glanced at Darcy. "I'm still disappointed that Josh won't be here," she said. "But, I have to admit, this is pretty cool."

"And we won't have to work as hard, either," Darcy agreed.

Normally all the Summer Sail members were kept busy. If they weren't checking the rigging, they were helping to run the sails or secure the lines. But tonight the motor did most of the work.

"Later tonight we'll learn about celestial navigation—steering by the stars," Ryan told them as the *Sunshine* made a slow circle around the harbor. "Old-time sailors always knew where to find Polaris, the North Star. It's the most important star to sail by."

Stephanie couldn't stop imagining what tonight would have been like if she and Josh had been able to be together. With a sigh she walked away from the group. She leaned against the railing and enjoyed the cool harbor breeze. She gazed across the bay.

*This would be extra beautiful—if I could share it with Josh,* she thought. *It's the perfect romantic setting.* She sighed and pushed a stray hair off her face. *Why isn't he here*? A terrible doubt crept into her thoughts. *Could he have decided he wanted to be with Darah after all?* she worried.

"You seem kind of down, Stephanie."

Stephanie jumped in surprise and whirled around. "Will you please stop coming up behind me like that?" she snapped at Ryan. "You scared me half to death!"

"Whoa!" Ryan said. "A little jumpy, aren't you? I was just worried about you. You're not your usual bouncy self. So sue me."

"Sorry," Stephanie mumbled. "I am kind of bummed. I was looking forward to spending tonight with Josh."

"Is that all? That's what you're moping about?" Ryan shook his head. "Stephanie, these overnights are fun, but they're work, too. What did you expect? Did you think this was going to be a private romantic cruise for just you and Josh? Was Josh going to serenade you under the stars or something?"

Stephanie felt her face heat up. "Of course not," she protested, even though that was sort of what she had hoped. Well, not the serenading part, exactly.

Ryan burst out laughing. "Well, if it's serenading you want . . ." He suddenly dropped to one knee. To Stephanie's horror, he burst into an off-key rendition of a corny old love song.

People who happened to be walking along the deck turned and stared.

"Cut it out," she hissed.

Ryan sang louder.

Stephanie spun around and stormed away. *This has to be the worst night of my life,* Stephanie thought.

Stephanie sat up with a yawn and stretched. Bright morning sunlight streamed in through the uncovered portholes.

"Not a bad night's sleep," she remarked. At least she would see Josh again today. And she could ask him what happened. Maybe there was a totally reasonable explanation.

She had to admit it was fun to be on the water at night—despite her disappointment. Once Ryan quit teasing her about Josh, that is.

"Let's grab breakfast," Allie said, jumping down from her bunk. "I'm starving!"

Stephanie and her friends quickly dressed and joined the others at breakfast. Stephanie helped herself to a big cup of orange juice and a corn muffin.

"A night on the water really gives you an appetite, doesn't it?" Sam remarked. He held up a plate that held two bagels and a muffin.

"Yeah. And having a late breakfast on board was a great idea," Stephanie added.

Sleeping on board also gave them a chance to finish their morning chores long before the others arrived for the day. They had plenty of free time until their morning lesson. Stephanie made sure to look especially nice for Josh. Soon it was time for their Summer Sail session to begin.

"Don't look now," Darcy said. "But here come our favorite sailors. The Flamingoes!"

"Hey, is Darah wearing a Zack and the Zees concert T-shirt?" Allie said, narrowing her eyes to see better. "I haven't seen that design before, have you, Stephanie?"

Stephanie shook her head no.

"Look at the date on it," Anna said. "It's from a concert last night!"

Stephanie shielded her eyes from the sun. "How can that be? I know the entire Zack and the Zees concert schedule. There was nothing planned for this area last night."

Darah strutted on board and nodded smugly at Stephanie and her friends. Now that Stephanie could see Darah close up, there was no question—Darah's T-shirt had last night's date on it.

But what Stephanie saw next made her heart do flip-flops.

Josh bounded up the gangplank—wearing an identical Zack and the Zees T-shirt.

"Oh, no!" Stephanie gasped. She turned to her friends and whispered, "Josh wasn't here last night because he went to that concert—with Darah!"

# CHAPTER 11

"Don't panic," Darcy ordered Stephanie. "We have to get to the bottom of this."

Darah grinned. "I see you are all admiring my new T-shirt," she said. "Well, if you like the T-shirt, you would have loved the concert. Zack and the Zees were the best last night."

"Where were Zack and the Zees playing?" Stephanie demanded. "We didn't hear anything about a concert."

Darah smirked at her. "Of course you didn't," she said. "But you did hear about the Boyz Town concert, right?"

Stephanie nodded, confused. "They played at the Golden Gate Park Summer Nights show. But what does Boyz Town have to do with anything?"

"Zack and the Zees were their surprise guests! Only it wasn't a surprise to me," Darah boasted. "My cousin works at a music magazine, and he told me about it. Someone leaked the news to them. But I told only very special friends," she added, nodding in Josh's direction.

Stephanie felt as though Darah had kicked her in the stomach. She could just picture how it happened. When Darah heard about Zack and the Zees, she had the perfect excuse to ask Josh to go to the concert. That was why Darah offered to switch nights with her. And, Stephanie realized miserably, that was the reason Josh never changed his work assignment. Because he would rather go to the concert with Darah than spend the evening on the boat with her.

"Well, time to sail," Darah said cheerfully. Tiffany, Mary, and Cynthia followed Darah as she strolled away.

Stephanie watched them go, too stunned to move.

"You know, technically Josh didn't ask her out, since she asked him," Darcy said, trying to console Stephanie.

"Maybe he didn't even want to go on a date

with her," Anna suggested. "Maybe he's just a big Zack and the Zees fan."

For a moment Stephanie brightened. But then she shook her head. "Bottom line, Josh chose Darah over me."

Kayla patted her shoulder sympathetically. Then the girls had to split up to join their teams.

As Stephanie hurried to meet her group, she passed Josh. He was leaning against the cabin wall, holding a clipboard. "Hello!" he called out.

"Hi," Stephanie replied, wishing she could just sneak by him. She hoped he wouldn't try to talk to her. She didn't trust herself not to reveal her disappointment. This was not her lucky day—Josh was headed straight for her.

"So did you have fun on your overnight?" Josh asked.

*No,* she wanted to reply. *Did you have fun on your date with Darah?* But instead she just mumbled, "It was okay."

"I went to an awesome concert last night," Josh continued. "I had my days confused and yesterday I thought the concert was Thursday, but really it was last night, so I didn't have to switch."

"I noticed," Stephanie said, pointing at the date on his T-shirt.

Josh glanced down, then laughed. "Oh, right," he said. "I forgot I was wearing it."

"So, are you a big Zack and the Zees fan?" Stephanie forced herself to sound normal.

"Sure am." He smiled broadly. "So it was doubly cool when they showed up at the Boyz Town concert. Man, I couldn't believe my luck."

Luck? "But—" Stephanie began to say. She felt confused. "But didn't you know about it in advance?"

Josh laughed again. "How could I? No one knew. That's why it's called a surprise."

"But Darah knew . . ." *And she said she told you,* Stephanie added silently. *This is so weird.*

"Did she? I wonder how. She didn't say anything when I ran into her at the concession stand. She just admired the T-shirt I bought."

*And Darah bought one to match. Just so she could make it look like she and Josh had gone to the concert together.* It was all making sense to Stephanie now. *That sneaky rat!*

"I'd better let you get to work," Josh said. "See you later." He saluted her with his clipboard.

She watched him amble away, her mood one hundred percent better. It didn't matter that he didn't switch nights. The only thing that mattered was that he didn't go on a date with Darah.

*And I am going to let her know I'm on to her! Darah is not going to get away with this.*

Stephanie scanned the deck until she spotted

Darah with the rest of the Flamingoes. Their friends Andrew and Mark were there, too. They were gathered by the headsail, probably waiting for their counselor.

Stephanie stalked up to Darah. "Listen, Darah," she fumed. "You're not fooling anyone—especially not me."

Darah raised an eyebrow and stared at Stephanie. "What are you talking about?"

"I know that you lied about going to the concert with Josh."

Darah shrugged. "Oh, that. Just having a little fun with you. You should have seen your face. It was priceless." Tiffany, Mary, and Cynthia snickered. Even Andrew and Mark chuckled.

Stephanie seethed with anger. Unbelievable! Darah didn't even care that Stephanie had caught her in a lie. "Well, you can cut the act," Stephanie said. "Because I know that Josh isn't the slightest bit interested in you. He likes *me*."

Darah's blue eyes narrowed. "Don't be so sure."

"I *am* sure," Stephanie insisted.

Darah rolled her eyes. "Oh, right. Your stupid so-called note. Big deal."

"It wasn't stupid and he *does* like me." Stephanie felt frustrated. *You sound like nine-year-old Michelle,* she scolded herself. *Stop it. You can't let Darah get to you like this.*

"Don't even think about it," she warned Darah. "He likes me, and that's that."

"Only because I haven't been trying," Darah taunted.

Stephanie clenched her fists so hard, she felt the nails dig into her palms. *Just walk away,* she ordered herself. She spun on her heel and hurried to find her crew.

Darah wasn't going to back off. *In fact,* Stephanie worried, *I may have just made things a whole lot worse.*

When all the Summer Sail kids had assembled, Josh gathered them around for a talk. "This is a big week for us," he said. "The regatta is a week from Saturday. And that gives us just a little more than a week to get ready."

The kids all let out a loud cheer. "We'll be ready!" someone shouted.

"Only three other programs are competing," Josh continued. "The Sausalito Yacht Club, the Marin County Yacht Club, and a club from Santa Cruz. Sausalito is the one to beat—they are a top-notch group!"

"I've heard of them," Kayla remarked.

Josh nodded. "The only way we'll win is if everyone pulls together. Everybody here has to support everybody else, no matter what. So, it's really up to all of you."

*Like I would ever be on the same team as a Flamingo,* Stephanie thought.

"First, let's review the emergency procedures we already learned," Josh continued. "We probably won't have any emergencies, but it's a good idea to be well drilled. Then, if something does go wrong, you can act quickly without needing to think about it."

The instructors walked all the groups through the procedures to follow if they were caught in a storm, or if someone fell overboard or got hurt.

Then they rotated through assignments as they sailed the course for the regatta. They steered the *Sunshine* around the same series of marker buoys again and again.

Stephanie and her crew were assigned to man the mainsail. Ryan gave the order to hoist, and Stephanie pulled on the line. At first the sail slid up smoothly—exactly as it was supposed to. Then the knot hit the big metal pulley that helped the rope slide. The rope caught and the sail stuck half-way up the mast.

"Hey!" Stephanie exclaimed. "What's going on here?" She yanked hard on the line, but the main-sail flapped uselessly. The boat drifted off course.

Lucy and Sam rushed over to help as Stephanie

attempted to fix the line. She heard kids shouting all over the boat, trying to find out what was going wrong.

Josh hurried over to see what was happening. He found the knot at once. "Stephanie, didn't you check the rigging before you hoisted the sail?" he asked.

"Well, no," Stephanie admitted. "But it didn't have a knot in it earlier."

Josh looked grim. "You have to do your job thoroughly," he scolded. "What if this happened during the regatta? What good would excuses be then?" he demanded.

Stephanie felt terrible. He was absolutely right. But she was sure there hadn't been a knot in the line before.

"I suggest you take down this rigging, untie that knot, and do the job right," Josh ordered. "Things were going very smoothly until now. Your mistake would have cost us the race."

He turned and went to confer with Fran. "Way to go," Ryan said sarcastically. "You made us all look like we didn't know how to do our jobs."

Stephanie felt terrible. "I'm really sorry," she apologized.

"I bet." Ryan reached up to begin taking down the rigging. "You're sorry you made Dreamboat mad at you."

"That's not it," Stephanie protested. She looked at the members of her group. "I want to do well in the regatta. All of us."

Ryan just grunted, and Lucy and Sam went to work. Stephanie glanced over to see if Josh was still steamed. She didn't see him. But she did see Darah smirking at her.

*Of course,* Stephanie thought, *that knot was no accident. That was another dirty trick by the Flamingoes.*

"I say we give as good as we get," Darcy declared. "This is war!"

The girls were on lunch break, trying to figure out what to do about Darah and the Flamingoes. Stephanie told them about the knot incident, and her friends were furious.

"It's terrible that Josh is mad at you because of Darah," Darcy complained.

"I know," Stephanie muttered. "She got exactly what she wanted. She made me look stupid *and* she spoiled things with Josh."

"I bet we could come up with much worse pranks to play on Darah," Kayla said, her eyes gleaming.

"Like emptying the bilge pump on her head," Darcy suggested.

"Or hoisting her up the mainsail," Anna added.

Stephanie snorted. "Why don't we just throw them all overboard?"

"Well, that might be a little tough," Allie said. "How about just Darah."

They all laughed. Then Stephanie became serious. "I don't think we should stoop to their level," she declared. "Especially since I know exactly what the best revenge would be . . ." She gazed at her friends. "To get Josh all for myself!"

"Stephanie, you were supposed to coil those lines!" Ryan barked at her.

Stephanie turned around and stared at the deck in dismay. The ropes that she had just spent twenty minutes carefully coiling and stowing lay in a tangled heap.

"But I—" she began to protest. Then she spotted Darah and Tiffany sneaking around the side of the cabin. Of course—another Darah special. "I'll take care of it." She sighed and dropped back down on the deck.

The whole afternoon, Darah and the Flamingoes managed to make Stephanie look stupid. The tangled ropes were just the last prank in a long line of petty sabotages. And what made everything so awful was that watching out for the Flamingoes made it hard for Stephanie to pay attention to what she was doing. She made mistakes she hadn't made since the first week.

The worst thing of all—Josh seemed to be so disappointed in her. "I thought you were a better sailor than that," he even commented as she accidentally pulled the wrong line. Everyone on board had the jitters about the upcoming regatta. Today's rotten practice race only made them more nervous.

*It wasn't just me messing up,* Stephanie recalled. The Flamingoes were so busy setting up their tricks that they left their posts and were slow to follow orders. Josh gave the entire crew a lecture about working together and then strode off the boat without even saying good-bye.

Finally Stephanie finished recoiling the ropes. She went below and grabbed her backpack. *That's weird,* she thought. *I'm sure I buckled the straps.* When she picked it up, an envelope fell out.

Stephanie's eyes opened wide. There on the envelope was the letter *S*—just like on the note that Josh had slipped inside her sweatshirt.

*Did Josh send me another note?* She snatched it up and eagerly tore it open. She felt so nervous that her fingers trembled. Her breath caught as she read the romantic words.

S—

It seems that Summer Sail is always getting

in the way of us having a chance to be alone together. I can't wait any longer to spend time with my special girl. Please meet me on the *Sunshine* at 7 P.M., the evening before the regatta. I intend to make it a night to remember.

Love,
Josh

"He's not mad at me after all!" Stephanie exclaimed. She stuffed the note back into her backpack. Who cared about Darah's silly pranks now? Josh liked her—he *really liked her!*

# CHAPTER 12

"You look great, Stephanie!" Aunt Becky exclaimed.

"I do, don't I?" Stephanie agreed, staring at her reflection in the mirror. She wore her favorite, most sophisticated outfit—a short, form-fitting silver dress and a small black choker with a silver heart charm on it. Aunt Becky helped her pile her long, blond hair into an elegant French twist.

Tonight was the night—her date with Josh right before the regatta. All week whenever she thought of his wonderful note and how he called her his special girl, she couldn't calm the butterflies fluttering in her stomach.

Stephanie left her house and walked as quickly

as she could in her high-heeled black sandals to the bus stop. She glanced up at the sky. It was turning a gorgeous shade of deep blue as the sun slipped below the horizon. *The same blue as Josh's eyes,* Stephanie noted.

She hopped on the bus for the short trip to the marina. *So many things could happen tonight,* she thought. *Maybe Josh has a romantic picnic laid out on the deck of the* Sunshine. *Or maybe he set up a huge bouquet of flowers for me. Or maybe*—she gasped. *Maybe he'll even kiss me!*

Soon the marina came into view. Stephanie stepped off the bus. The cool breeze coming off the water felt wonderful on her skin as she made her way toward the *Sunshine.*

She skipped a few steps before she caught herself. She giggled as she glanced around, hoping no one had seen her. Luckily the pier was deserted.

Before her, the *Sunshine* creaked as it rocked gently in the water. With each step she took up the gangplank, Stephanie could feel her heart thump harder and harder in her chest.

She boarded the boat. Strange. It seemed completely empty. Stephanie walked up and down the deck. No sign of Josh anywhere.

*I know he wrote me to meet him here,* she thought. Puzzled, she stood at the top of the stairs leading down into the galley. "Josh?" she called softly. "Are you there?"

No response.

Stephanie's heart sank. Could it be that he had a change of heart? Maybe he wasn't going to show up at all!

"Josh?" she called again, louder this time.

"Stephanie!" Josh's voice replied. "Down here!"

*Yes! He is here!* Stephanie felt joy rush through her. She ran down the steps into the galley. "Oh, Josh, I . . ."

Stephanie stopped dead in her tracks. Standing in the galley was not only Josh, but the entire Summer Sail crew, minus her group of friends. "Wh-what's going on here?" Stephanie stammered.

"I was about to ask you the same thing," Josh responded. "You're pretty dressed up for our last meeting before the regatta."

"Meeting?" Stephanie squeaked. "What are you talking about? What meeting?"

"The crew is spending the evening making sure the *Sunshine* is in tip-top shape. Scrubbing and polishing everything for tomorrow's race," Josh explained.

Stephanie looked over the crowd. Everyone was dressed in raggedy old clothes. She felt completely out of place in her short silver dress.

Darah stepped up to Stephanie. *"Somehow,*

Stephanie and her friends must not have heard about the meeting. I wonder how they all missed the news?" She gave Stephanie a wicked smirk.

"Well, she certainly can't scrub anything in *those* clothes," Tiffany put in. "What's up, Stephie? Have a hot date with someone?"

Then Darah, Tiffany, Mary, and Cynthia snickered among themselves.

"But, Josh, I thought we—" Stephanie began to say. But she was cut off by the sound of a chuckle from the far end of the room. Then another. Soon all the kids were laughing at Stephanie.

Her cheeks flaming, Stephanie blinked back tears of embarrassment.

"Oh, *special girl,*" Darah taunted, "this truly has been a night to remember, hasn't it?"

Stephanie stared at Darah, the full impact of what Darah had done finally hit her.

They set her up. Josh never wrote her that note at all. It was just a horrible Flamingo prank. The meanest one they ever pulled.

All Stephanie wanted to do was throw herself at Darah and rip out all her auburn hair by the roots. Instead, she turned and fled from the *Sunshine,* tears streaming down her face.

"Stephanie! Wait!" she heard Josh call as she ran back to the marina entrance. But she couldn't turn back. She was too hurt. To embarrassed to let Josh see her like this.

She jumped on the bus waiting at the marina gate. As it pulled away, Stephanie vowed one thing. There was no way she would let Darah get away with what she'd done. She was going to pay—and pay big.

# CHAPTER 13

"That's the most horrible thing I've ever heard!" Allie exclaimed.

All of Stephanie's friends had gathered around her at the *Sunshine* early the next morning. The sky was gray and the wind whipped Stephanie's ponytail violently behind her. *The day seems angry,* Stephanie thought. *Almost as angry as I am.*

"I can't believe even Darah would stoop that low," Anna agreed. "She is absolutely the most horrible person on the face of the earth."

"Tell me about it," Stephanie muttered.

"There's no way we can let those Flamingoes get away with this!" Darcy exclaimed.

"Don't worry, we won't," Allie told her. "But

there's nothing we can do about this right now. We have to race in the regatta. We have to work with the Flamingoes. If we don't, the *Sunshine* might lose!"

"Teammates with the Flamingoes." Kayla shuddered. "I can't think of anything more repulsive."

"Allie's right. If we fight them now, we'll just look even worse to Josh and the rest of the crew," Stephanie pointed out. "We have to try our best to remember the regatta, and forget the Flamingoes—for now."

Darcy, Allie, Anna, and Kayla agreed to give it their best shot. "But if any of those Flamingoes get in my face," Stephanie added, "I can't promise anything."

Soon the rest of the Summer Sail crew began arriving. Josh and Ryan stepped on the boat. Together they began psyching everyone up for the big race.

Josh made eye contact with Stephanie. *Oh, no.* Stephanie thought. *I'm too embarrassed to talk to him now!*

But Josh strode right up to her. "Hey, Steph," he said.

"Hey," Stephanie replied. She kept her eyes glued to the deck.

"Listen," Josh went on softly, "I don't know

what happened between you and Darah last night. All I know is, it seemed pretty horrible."

"It was," Stephanie admitted.

"I'm really sorry about that. Honestly. And later, if you want, we can talk about it. But whatever it was, let's try to keep it on land, just for today, okay?"

"Sure, Josh." Stephanie gave him a halfhearted smile.

"Hey, come on," Josh said, and gazed deeply into Stephanie's eyes. "You're still my number-one sailor. I'm counting on you."

Stephanie felt a full smile fill her face. Maybe what the Flamingoes did didn't matter that much after all. Even if Darah made her feel horrible last night, Josh still seemed to like her. That made her feel more than a bit better.

"Aye-aye, captain. Number-one sailor on duty," she told him.

"That's my girl." Josh squeezed Stephanie's shoulder. "We'll be under way in a few minutes." He turned and looked over his shoulder. "Hey, Sam! How's it going, man?" Josh crossed the deck to talk to Sam.

"How are you feeling now?" Allie asked.

Steph turned to answer, and the smile faded from her face. "I *was* feeling great." She pointed over Allie's shoulder. "Until *they* showed up."

Darah, Tiffany, Cynthia, and Mary flounced on board the *Sunshine*. Darah glanced over at Stephanie, then led her group far off into the bow of the boat.

*Good idea, Darah,* Stephanie thought. *Just keep all your little pink-feathered friends on the other side of the boat, and we won't have any trouble.*

Soon Josh put everyone to work. Ryan was so keyed up about the regatta that he didn't bother teasing Stephanie about anything. *Which is good,* Stephanie thought. *Because if he says a single teasing word to me, I might not be able to control my temper.*

Steph ignored the amused looks she was getting from some of the other Summer Sail kids. When she passed Kayla on her way to stow the sail cover, her friend encouraged her with a smile.

"Hang in there," Kayla said.

"I'm trying," Stephanie replied.

"Stephanie! Stephanie! Over here!"

Stephanie glanced to shore when she heard her name. A huge crowd of spectators had gathered on the lawn of the yacht club. Stephanie spotted Michelle jumping up and down and waving frantically. She was standing with D.J., Jesse, Joey, and the twins. She could see Jesse pointing her out to Nicky and Alex.

"Stephanie! Over here!" Michelle called again, her voice carried by the strong wind.

Stephanie grinned and waved back.

"She sees us!" Nicky screamed.

Everywhere she looked she saw people sitting in chairs or sprawled on picnic blankets. Brightly colored pennants flapped in the breeze overhead. More pennants were draped around the speaker stand that was set up at the edge of the dock nearest the clubhouse. Stephanie felt her pulse race as excitement surged through her.

She turned to her friends. "This *is* pretty awesome," she admitted.

Darcy readjusted her backward baseball cap. "Know what? I think this is going to be fantastic."

"Did you see your family?" Kayla asked.

"They're right up front." Stephanie pointed them out. "How about you?"

Kayla shook her head. "There are too many people. I can't see them."

"I never expected such a huge turnout," Allie commented.

"It's because *we're* competing this year," Anna joked.

"Shhh," Darcy said. "Josh is trying to say something."

Stephanie turned around. Josh was having trouble getting everyone to settle down. Stephanie could feel the excitement running through the crew like a surge of electric current.

"I know you're all really buzzed about the race," he told them with a broad smile. "Just remember everything we worked on this past month. You've become great sailors, every one of you! Now it's time to trust yourselves, to use what you know. It should be instinctive by now." He grinned. "And listen to orders, of course!"

Everybody laughed.

Stephanie squeezed Allie's hand. "This is *sooo* exciting!" Allie whispered.

"Okay, crew members, find your group leaders," Josh told them. "And take your positions!"

Everyone scattered to their posts. Stephanie, Darcy, and Lucy had been assigned to work the mainsail. Ryan and Fran were helping. Darah and Cynthia were stationed next to them with Jenny.

*Great,* Stephanie thought miserably. *Why does Darah have to be practically on top of me?*

"Get ready," Josh called from his spot at the helm.

The loudspeakers over the marina crackled as Craig bounded onto the speaker stand and began his announcements.

"Ladies and gentlemen, children, friends, and guests. Welcome to the Bay Area Regatta. We're honored by the presence of some really tough sailors today. The Sausalito Yacht Club, the Marin County Yacht Club, the Santa Cruz Yacht

Club—and, of course, our own Golden Gate Yacht Club." Wild applause greeted the mention of each team.

"This race follows a tricky course marked by buoys in the harbor area," Craig explained. "The first boat to successfully complete the course wins our highest honor—this gold trophy." Craig hoisted the huge, impressive trophy over his head. The crowd whistled and cheered. Stephanie was sure she could hear her family shouting louder than everyone else.

Stephanie glanced over at Darah. Once again she groaned inwardly. *I can't believe I'm going to have to look at her for the whole race.*

*Boom!*

Stephanie's thoughts were interrupted by the firing of the starting gun.

"Stephanie! Darah! To your stations!" Ryan shouted.

The *Sunshine* pulled easily away from her starting position. The other boats also moved smoothly across the harbor.

"Ryan, what are our chances?" Stephanie asked. "Do you think we can win?"

Ryan glanced at the sky. "The wind could be a problem," Ryan answered. "Can you feel it? We could get a really stiff blowup anytime. The wind can whip up suddenly in the bay."

"Coming about!" Josh shouted.

They all worked together, ducking the swinging boom and securing their lines as Josh steered the *Sunshine* around the first marker buoy.

Stephanie suddenly saw the *Saucy Susan,* manned by the Sausalito team, pulling ahead on their starboard side.

She gaped at the boat, openmouthed. "How did they do that?" she called to Ryan.

"Angle of the sail," Ryan called back in a clipped voice. "They caught good wind. Tighten your line!"

Stephanie leaped to obey. At the same moment Darah backed away from the cleat where she had secured the end of her line.

"Watch it!" Stephanie shouted. "You nearly knocked me over." She stumbled as she reached to secure the mainsail rope.

Ryan grabbed it from her. "What do you think you're doing?" he yelled at Darah and Stephanie.

"Sorry!" Darah scowled at Stephanie. "It was an accident."

"Oh, I believe that," Stephanie replied in a sarcastic tone.

"Cut it out," Ryan ordered. "You two could have made us go off course. Now, pay attention. I don't like this wind at all."

Stephanie realized that the wind *was* whipping up. A moment before the water had been slightly choppy. Now the *Sunshine* began rolling and slapping down in larger waves.

Saltwater spray shot into the air and splashed over the sides of the *Sunshine*.

Lucy was green. "I was afraid of this," she gulped.

Ryan took one glance and ordered her into the cabin. Then he took over both his line and Lucy's. The wind blew across the deck with a roar. He had to shout to be heard. "Shorten the sails!" he ordered.

Stephanie grabbed the mainsail line and loosened it. It was wet with spray and pulled roughly against her palms. Instead of being able to pull it up tighter, she felt it slip through her fingers.

She glanced around in a panic. "I can't hold on!"

"You jerk!" Darah shouted. "You can't even do your own job."

"Be quiet," Stephanie yelled back. "I don't even want you to talk to me."

"Oh, I'm so upset." Darah sneered and took a step away from her position. The *Sunshine* pitched forward and into a deep, sickening roll to the starboard side. A huge wave crashed over the railing.

"Darah!" Ryan shouted. "Get back to your post!" He turned away to work Lucy's line.

Darah was moving when the boat pitched again and a huge wall of water shot over the deck.

Stephanie watched in horror as Darah was washed overboard.

# CHAPTER 14

"Man overboard!" Stephanie shouted into the roar of the wind. "Man overboard!"

*Did anyone hear me?*

She glanced into the wild waves, straining for a glimpse of Darah. The *Sunshine* had pulled ahead of the spot where Darah fell in.

Stephanie glanced behind her and saw that Fran had already joined Ryan at the mainsail. Together they hauled on the crank to shorten the wet line. The *Sunshine* continued to bounce and roll on the waves, but slowly the boat turned and headed back toward Darah.

Tiffany and Cynthia ran to the side of the boat

to catch a glimpse of their friend. "What did you do?" Tiffany screamed at Stephanie.

"Nothing! I didn't do anything!" Stephanie protested.

"I'll bet you didn't," Cynthia yelled.

Stephanie glanced at the wall next to her. A life preserver! She grabbed it and flung it over the side toward Darah. It landed with a splash. She thought she saw Darah swimming toward it.

*But what if she can't make it?* Stephanie thought. She bit her lip, worried. Darah had given her plenty of trouble. But that didn't mean she could stand by and watch her drown!

"We're getting closer to her!" Josh yelled. "Grab the lifeline!"

Darcy, Ryan, Jenny, Cynthia, and Tiffany ran to grasp the, heavy line that was attached to the life preserver. Together they managed to pull Darah closer to the boat. They could drag Darah in faster than she could swim.

Stephanie remembered Ryan saying how hard it was to swim through rough water. "You get tired really fast when you're panicked—and fighting for your life," he said during one of their emergency drills.

"Darah! Darah!" Stephanie shouted.

The sudden wind had whipped the waves even

higher. She lost sight of the white life preserver—and Darah.

Without thinking, Stephanie scrambled over the railing and swung onto the metal ladder that ran down the side of the boat.

Clinging to the ladder, she lowered herself onto the bottom rung.

"There she is!" someone yelled.

Stephanie spotted Darah only two feet away. Up on deck, Darcy, Jenny, Ryan, and Tiffany pulled even harder on the lifeline.

"Stephanie! What are you doing?" Josh screamed. "Climb back up here! Now!"

"I can reach her! I can save her!" Stephanie yelled back over the crashing of the waves.

She leaned out as far as she could.

"Easy!" Josh yelled. "Hold on tight!"

"Don't worry," Stephanie shouted back. "I'm okay!"

Darah was only inches away. Stephanie stretched toward her. "Grab my hand!" she yelled.

For a split second Darah hesitated. Stephanie stared at her.

"Don't be stupid! I don't care about the tricks you pulled. Grab my hand. Now!" Stephanie ordered.

Darah threw herself forward at the same time that the lifeline yanked her in.

"Yes!" Stephanie grunted as Darah's fingers wrapped around hers. She pulled as hard as she could. A wave swept Darah against the metal ladder.

Stephanie grabbed her, wrapping one arm around her waist. Darah managed to clutch a rung. Then she seemed to collapse.

Just in time, Jenny and Ryan leaned over and reached under Darah's arms. At the same moment, Darcy and Tiffany pulled again on the lifeline.

Darah was half dragged up the rest of the way.

Stephanie gulped down a few deep breaths. She felt exhausted. Definitely too tired to climb the rest of the way up the short ladder.

She was suddenly grateful for the life jacket she wore. *Just in case,* she thought. *I know I won't fall in, but just in case . . .*

A second later she felt strong arms wrap around her. Ryan and Jenny hoisted her toward the deck and helped her climb up over the railing.

"Where's Darah?" she gasped out.

"She's okay," Ryan told her. "She's cold and wet and tired, but she'll be fine. Thanks to you," he added with a grin.

Stephanie grinned back. *It's funny,* she realized. *I am totally happy that Darah is okay. All the Flamingoes' tricks don't matter. Not at all. They're not important anymore.*

Then she felt the boat lurch beneath her feet. She stumbled into Ryan.

"Jetty!" she heard Josh shout.

Ryan tossed his hair out of his eyes and peered starboard. "Oh, no! We're heading right for a rock jetty!"

Stephanie gasped. "The boat will be smashed to bits!"

# CHAPTER 15

Stephanie hurried to her position at the mainsail. She hesitated for a moment, then rushed over to the Flamingoes at the jib.

"Listen," she declared. "You don't like me and I don't like you. But if we don't work together, we're going to crash."

"We don't take orders from you," Tiffany retorted.

Stephanie ran her hands though her dripping hair in exasperation. "Aren't you listening?" she demanded. "We could drown!"

"Stephanie's right," Darah said. Stephanie turned around to see the Flamingo leader standing behind her. She had changed into a pair of dry shorts and sweatshirt. "We have to work together as a team."

She and Stephanie gazed at each other, then nodded. Stephanie figured now that Darah was back at her post, she would let *her* worry about her Flamingo friends. Shivering in her wet clothes, Stephanie raced back to work the mainsail. They managed to control the luffing and finally were able to steer the boat away from the deadly jetty. Once the boat was out of danger, Ryan ordered her below to find dry clothes.

Jenny went with her, leading her into the girls' cabin. She helped her peel off her soaking wet clothes and get her wrapped in a warm blanket.

"I'll find you some dry clothes," Jenny said. She disappeared but was back in a minute with somebody's oversized sweatpants, T-shirt, and sweatshirt. Stephanie climbed into them. She did her best to dry her hair, then hurried back on deck.

"I look pretty dumb, don't I?" she asked Ryan, glancing down at the clothes that hung around her body.

"Not bad for a drowned rat," Ryan teased. "A very brave drowned rat," he added with a smile.

"Too bad we're going to lose this race," Darah commented from her post.

"Lose?" Stephanie frowned. "I didn't risk my life to come in last!" she declared.

"Me neither," Darah said.

Ryan heard them and laughed out loud. "Tell you what—let's give it all we've got. No way we can win this thing, but we can show them the stuff we're made of!"

"Right," Stephanie agreed. "We're not giving up without a fight!" She and Ryan slapped high-fives. Then they went to tell the rest of the crew.

"Okay," Josh told them as they gathered at the helm. "We totally lost all headway. I'm going to have to back the mainsail."

He shouted instructions at Fran, Ryan, and Jenny.

Stephanie helped Fran and Darcy hoist the mainsail back to its full height. In a few minutes the *Sunshine* was back on course and racing forward at top speed. They ripped ahead so fast, the boat tilted sideways.

The *Sunshine* tacked back and forth as it approached the final mark.

"Coming about!" Josh yelled as he turned into the wind.

As they crossed the finish line, a wild burst of applause rang out from the entire marina.

"Why are they cheering? We lost!" Darah exclaimed.

"They're cheering because you're all winners," Josh told her. "You all pulled together as a team.

You showed you were tough and that you cared. And in the end, that's what really counts."

Stephanie threw her arms around Darcy's neck. "I'm so proud of all of us!" she exclaimed.

"That was the wildest thing I've ever done," Darcy remarked as the *Sunshine* tied up in her slip. "I've never been so excited and scared all at once."

Television crews swarmed around them as the crew disembarked. Flashbulbs blinded Stephanie as reporters took pictures.

"Oh, it was terrifying," Stephanie heard Darah saying into a reporter's microphone. "One of the crew lost control of a sail, and when I went to help, I was swept overboard. Thank goodness I'm a strong swimmer. Otherwise I would never have been able to save myself."

Stephanie rolled her eyes. *Leave it to Darah to forget that we all saved her.*

"Honey, are you okay?" Stephanie's dad wrapped her in a big hug. The crew of *Wake Up, San Francisco* was interviewing the winning team nearby.

"I'm fine," Stephanie reassured him. "In fact, it was the greatest!"

"You gave us all a scare!" Danny said, rubbing her back. "Are you sure you're warm enough?"

"I promise I'm okay, Dad." Stephanie's eyes roamed the crowd, searching for Josh. She wanted to share this amazing moment with him. True, they didn't win the regatta, but it was an awesome experience anyway.

She spotted his golden hair in the sun. "Excuse me," she told her dad. "There's someone I have to see."

She hurried over to where Josh stood on the clubhouse lawn. Then she noticed that Darah was also heading straight toward him. She couldn't believe it! Even after being saved by Stephanie on the boat, Darah couldn't let the competition over Josh drop.

It figured!

Then Stephanie froze in her tracks. So did Darah.

Both girls gasped.

# CHAPTER 16

A pretty, red-haired girl was throwing her arms around Josh's neck.

Then he kissed her! A long, passionate kiss.

Stephanie and Darah stood, openmouthed. Quickly, though, Darah spun on her heel and vanished into the crowd.

Stephanie couldn't move. She felt as if her feet were glued to the ground. Josh glanced up and noticed Stephanie watching.

He said something to the beautiful college-age girl and then jogged over to Stephanie.

"You did great," he said, congratulating her. He draped an arm across her shoulders and squeezed her tightly.

"Th-thanks," Stephanie stammered. *What is going on? Who is that girl?*

"Listen, I want you to meet my girlfriend, Stacy. I've told her a lot about you."

Stephanie's stomach tightened. *He has a girlfriend? And her name is Stacy,* she told herself, trying to grasp the situation. Then a deep suspicion welled inside her. "Stacy?" she repeated.

Josh gave her a puzzled look. "Yes. Stacy Travers. Why? Do you know her?"

Stephanie shook her head as she rummaged through her backpack. She pulled Josh's note out and showed it to him. "Is this note for Stacy?"

"Yes," Josh said. His brow wrinkled in confusion. "Why do *you* have it?"

"It was in the sweatshirt you lent me. I guess I accidentally read it," Stephanie said. "See? The initial of her first name is *S*. Just like mine."

"Oh." Josh took the note from her, and Stephanie saw the color rise in his cheeks. "No one was supposed to read that except Stacy."

"Sorry," Stephanie mumbled. She felt terrible.

"It's not your fault," he assured her. Then he smacked his forehead. "Oh, no. And you thought . . ."

"Oh, no," Stephanie said. "I knew the note wasn't for me. I mean, we're just friends—right?" She had to lie. There was no way she could tell him what she really thought. It was way too embarrassing.

"Right," Josh said with a smile. "See you later." Then he grabbed Stacy's hand and hurried off toward the clubhouse.

Stephanie stood and watched her Mr. Perfect—her destiny guy—leave with another girl.

"I've never seen the marina look so beautiful!" Stephanie stared at the twinkling white lights that outlined the shape of the clubhouse. The club had been lavishly decorated for the post-regatta party. More lights were strung overhead. They seemed to be reflected off the water in the harbor.

"Looks like it will be a fun dance, too," Allie said. She tapped her foot in time to the band playing on the front patio. Nearby, tables were stacked high with drinks and snacks.

"You look great, Al," Stephanie told her. "That blue fabric really sets off your hair color."

"Everyone looks great," Allie answered. "I love that deep green on you, Darce."

Darcy's dress had thin spaghetti straps and a trim of tiny black braid around the neckline. Kayla looked terrific in a short pink off-the-shoulder dress.

Anna had put together her usual dramatic outfit—a long red skirt, a black halter top, and a fringed shawl draped around her hips.

"And you look every bit as gorgeous as Stacy," Anna told Stephanie.

"You think so? Thanks!" Stephanie beamed. She had borrowed the shimmering deep-purple dress from D.J. It was form-fitting and totally sophisticated. The color positively glowed against her blond hair and blue eyes.

"So do you still believe in fate?" Darcy asked.

Stephanie thought for a moment. "You know, I think I do. I just got the signals crossed. Josh may not have turned out to be my destiny guy, but that doesn't mean Mr. Perfect isn't out there."

"Hey, here comes Ryan." Darcy poked Stephanie in the side. "Whoa—he looks great!"

Stephanie gaped at him in surprise. She realized she had never seen Ryan in anything but grub clothes, with his hair falling into his eyes. Tonight he wore spotless faded jeans and a beautiful linen blazer. They really showed off his height and his broad shoulders. His usually messy hair was brushed smoothly back.

"Steph!" Ryan called out as he came closer. "Wow! You look fantastic!"

"You look totally cool yourself!" she replied.

"You never would have believed it, right?" Ryan

joked. "But thanks. At least that proves you don't hate me or anything."

"I don't hate you," she told him. Then she giggled. "Okay, well, I guess, sometimes I did."

"I know," Ryan replied. "I suppose I went a little too far with all the teasing."

"Yeah, you did," Stephanie agreed. "I can't figure out why you were always picking on me."

"You can't really?" Ryan looked embarrassed. "Remember the first time you talked to me on the pier? I thought you were really cute."

"You made my life miserable because you thought I was cute?" Stephanie asked.

"Right. I mean, no! I mean—oh, it's going to sound really stupid."

"Stupid's okay," Stephanie told him. "I've been pretty stupid myself lately."

"I wanted to be able to spend more time with you, but you were always drooling over Josh."

"Sorry about that," Stephanie said.

Ryan sighed. "All the girls go crazy for him, and I was afraid he'd like you back. I mean, why wouldn't he?"

"Well, he has a girlfriend, for starters," Stephanie said. "But I'll take that as a compliment."

Ryan smiled at her. "If I had known about Stacy, I would have had a lot less to worry about."

"And maybe you would have been a lot less hard on me!" Stephanie teased.

"Well, that's all water under the bridge," Ryan quipped. "Get it?"

Stephanie groaned. "No more bad jokes, please!"

The band began playing a loud, fast song. Everyone began to dance.

"I promise not to make any more bad jokes if you'll dance with me."

"That's a deal," Stephanie said with a smile. They headed for the dance floor,

"Hey—you're not a bad dancer," Stephanie told Ryan.

"You either," he replied happily. "So, Stephanie, would you go out with me sometime?"

"I don't know," she said warily. "I don't know how long you can stand to be nice to me."

Ryan laughed. "You're right! We might have to have very short dates."

"Especially since we'd have to have a no-bad-jokes rule."

Ryan shook his head. "You drive a hard bargain."

Stephanie gazed up at Ryan. He was cute and he was funny, but she knew deep inside that he wasn't her Mr. Perfect. She would be happy to be friends with Ryan, but that was all.

She twirled around on the dance floor, taking in all the colors and sparkling lights.

*And that means that Mr. Perfect is still out there waiting for me.*

The summer had barely begun. She had plenty of time to search for her destiny guy. She smiled. *Ready or not, Mr. Perfect, here I come!*